THE
HISTORY
KEEPERS
CIRCUS MAXIMUS

www.**randomhousechildrens**.co.uk

THE
HISTORY
KEEPERS
CIRCUS MAXIMUS

DAMIAN DIBBEN

DOUBLEDAY

THE HISTORY KEEPERS: CIRCUS MAXIMUS
A DOUBLEDAY BOOK 978 0 857 53057 8

Published in Great Britain by Doubleday,
an imprint of Random House Children's Publishers UK
A Random House Group Company

This edition published 2012

1 3 5 7 9 10 8 6 4 2

Copyright © Damian Dibben, 2012
Front cover artwork © Steve Stone, 2012

The Random House Group Limited supports the Forest Stewardship Council (FSC®),
the leading international forest certification organization. Our books carrying the FSC
label are printed on FSC®-certified paper. FSC is the only forest certification scheme
endorsed by the leading environmental organizations, including Greenpeace. Our paper
procurement policy can be found at www.randomhouse.co.uk/environment.

RANDOM HOUSE CHILDREN'S PUBLISHERS UK
61–63 Uxbridge Road, London W5 5SA

www.**randomhousechildrens**.co.uk
www.**totallyrandombooks**.co.uk
www.**randomhouse**.co.uk

Addresses for companies within The Random House Group Limited can be found at:
www.randomhouse.co.uk/offices.htm

THE RANDOM HOUSE GROUP Limited Reg. No. 954009

A CIP catalogue record for this book is available from the British Library.

Printed and bound in the UK by Clays Ltd, St Ives plc

For the mad and marvellous
Morrisons of Derw Mill

1 THE QUEEN OF THE NIGHT

The night Jake Djones brought total disgrace upon himself and jeopardized the very survival of the History Keepers' Secret Service was so unnaturally, bitterly cold that the Baltic Sea almost froze over.

From the rocky, windswept shores of Denmark in the west to the frozen remoteness of Finland in the north, an endless expanse of ice – as thin as gossamer and a ghostly silver in the moonlight – curved across the horizon. A continual dusting of soft snow seemed to silence this far corner of the Earth in an otherworldly hush.

A ship with blue sails broke through the veneer of ice even as it was forming, heading for the twinkling lights of Stockholm – a fairytale archipelago of bays, promontories and islets.

The ship was called the *Tulip*, and at the creaking wheel stood a tall figure in a long fur coat. He reached out an elegant gloved hand and rang the bell. 'It's time, gentlemen,' he announced in a soft Charleston drawl.

Immediately two more silhouettes, both well wrapped up, came out of the snowy darkness and joined him at the helm, followed by a brightly coloured bird – a parrot – who nestled, shivering, on his master's shoulders. They gazed out eagerly through the snow as the ship sailed on towards the port. Their faces were slowly illuminated . . .

The figure in fur was strikingly handsome, a smile playing across his chiselled face. Next to him stood the owner of the parrot – a shorter boy with spectacles, his brows raised in a studious frown. The last person had olive skin, curly dark hair and big brown eyes that blinked with excitement. Three intrepid adolescents, young agents of the History Keepers' Secret Service: Nathan Wylder, Charlie Chieverley . . . and Jake Djones.

Charlie was the first to speak. 'Head for that central island there,' he said, pointing towards a group of spires and towers. 'That's Stadsholmen, Stockholm's old town – the grand jewel of these

2

islands, centre of the Swedish Empire. Though sadly, of course, we're not arriving in the city's heyday. In 1710 our old friend the plague came here, taking out nearly a third of the population.'

'Not arriving in its heyday?' drawled Nathan, pulling his coat tighter against the snow. 'That's putting it mildly. Sweden in the winter of 1782 has got to be the most inhospitable place in history.' He produced a tiny box from his pocket and applied lip salve. 'If my lips get any drier, they'll fall off.'

'Hell's bells, Nathan, '92!' Charlie exclaimed, closing his eyes and clenching his teeth in annoyance. 'We're in 1792. Honestly, I sometimes wonder how you made it this far.' Mr Drake – that was the name of his pet parrot – squawked in agreement, puffing up his feathers indignantly at the American.

'I'm pulling your leg.' Nathan smirked. 'Do you really think I'd be wearing this ankle-length sable coat in 1782? Not to mention these buckle-less riding boots – so austere they're practically Napoleonic.' He turned to Jake. 'The 1790s are all about dressing down.' Nathan loved clothes almost as much as he loved an adventure.

'Buckle-less riding boots, my aunt,' Charlie

muttered to himself. 'And don't even get me started on your sable coat. It's a work of barbaric savagery. Those poor animals had the right to a life as well, you know.'

As Jake listened to their banter, he felt a great swelling of pride at the thought that he belonged to the greatest and most mysterious organization of all time: the History Keepers' Secret Service.

Just a month had passed since his life had changed for ever. He had been kidnapped, taken to the London bureau and informed that his parents had been secretly working for the service for decades – and indeed had gone missing in sixteenth-century Italy!

From then on it had been a nonstop roller-coaster ride. He had travelled through time, first to Point Zero – the History Keepers' headquarters on the Mont St Michel in Normandy, 1820 – and then to Venice in 1506, as part of the mission to find his mum and dad, and to stop the diabolical Prince Zeldt from destroying Europe with bubonic plague.

He had been reunited with his folks – but they had left behind Topaz, the mysterious and beautiful young agent to whom he had become devoted.

Most extraordinary of all, he had discovered that his beloved brother Philip, who had apparently died in an accident abroad three years ago, had also been a History Keeper; there was a chance – a very slim chance – that he was actually alive somewhere in the past.

And now Jake was already on his second mission. Admittedly he had been selected more through luck than anything else (nearly everyone at Point Zero had come down with an appalling tummy bug after eating mussel soup, and agents were thin on the ground), and it was not a dangerous assignment – otherwise he would definitely not have been included, as he was still a novice. But nonetheless here he was, travelling to the Baltic in the 1790s to collect a consignment of atomium, the precious liquid that made travelling through history possible.

'So, tell me something about the person we're meeting,' he said, trying to hide the tremor in his voice.

'Caspar Isaksen the Third?' Charlie shrugged. 'Not personally acquainted, but he's our age, I believe. I cooked a pumpkin tagine for his father once. He said it would live with him for ever.' Charlie loved food with a passion and was an expert cook – although an experience in the kitchens of Imperial Paris had left him a staunch vegetarian.

'*I've* been personally acquainted with Caspar Isaksen the Third. Twice,' drawled Nathan with a roll of his eyes. 'You can't really miss him – he eats cakes like they're going out of fashion, and never stops sneezing.'

'So what is the Isaksens' connection with atomium?' Jake persisted. He had learned all about this substance on his first voyage. To travel to a particular point in the past, agents had to drink a dilution of it, mixed with exact precision. Generally it worked only out at sea, in the magnetic maelstrom of a *horizon point*; and then only on the few humans with *valour* – an innate ability to travel through the ages. The History Keepers needed this precious liquid in order to watch over history, protecting the past from dark forces that sought to destroy it and plunge the world into darkness.

'The Isaksens *are* atomium,' replied Charlie. 'The family have been in charge of its production for more than two hundred years. As you know, it's notoriously tricky to make. To produce an effective batch, its ingredients – which themselves are kept a secret from all but a handful of keepers – have to be refined over a period of years . . .'

'Decades, I'd say,' Nathan added.

'Quite,' Charlie continued, 'and it must be created in freezing conditions. That's why Sejanus Poppoloe, the founder of the History Keepers, set up the laboratory in northern Sweden. After he had done so, back in the 1790s, he handed duties over to Frederick Isaksen, the first of the line. To this very day, *all* atomium – as used by every bureau in the world – has been created in the Isaksens' laboratory.'

'So, why are we meeting in Stockholm and not at the actual laboratory?' Jake asked.

'Dear me,' Charlie sighed, 'you *have* got a lot to learn. No one goes to the laboratory. *No one* has the slightest idea where it is, not even Commander Goethe.'

Jake stared back in surprise. Surely if anyone knew where the laboratory was based, it would be Galliana Goethe – the commander of the History Keepers for the past three years.

'Only the Isaksens keep the secret and pass it on,' Charlie continued. 'Can you imagine the disaster if its location got into the wrong hands? Catastrophe times infinity!'

'There's a myth,' Nathan said, 'that it's set within

a mountain, accessed through a secret limestone cave.'

'In any case,' Charlie concluded, 'when the atomium is ready, a member of the family delivers it to a prearranged location. As Caspar Isaksen is a fan of the opera, like me, the opera house was the venue chosen on this occasion. And not a moment too soon,' he added sombrely. 'Atomium stocks at Point Zero are at an all-time low. This consignment is vital.'

'So no slip-ups from the new boy,' Nathan said mischievously, thumping Jake on the back.

Jake looked around at the port. There were ships everywhere, an intricate forest of masts and rigging. Along the shore, depots and warehouses teemed with activity as sailors and tradesmen, their breath visible in the freezing air, worked into the evening, loading and unloading their cargoes: iron, copper and tin; crates of wax, resin and amber; sacks of rye and wheat; consignments of animal furs; and endless boxes of shining fish. Mr Drake surveyed the bustle with a keen eye, always intrigued – and just a touch nervous – when arriving at a new destination.

The *Tulip* docked in a narrow berth next to

a huge warship. Jake and Nathan gawped up at her great rounded hull punctuated by two cannon decks. High up on her starboard side a cluster of sailors, thick-necked and shaven-headed, stood talking in gruff voices.

Nathan caught their eye and lifted his fur hat in a flamboyant gesture. 'Lovely evening for the opera, wouldn't you say?' The sailors ignored him completely.

'You be a good boy and stay here.' Charlie stroked Mr Drake and gave him some peanuts. 'We shan't be long.' The parrot watched the three young agents jump down onto the quay.

They pulled their coats tight and, stepping carefully across the icy cobbles, made their way through the bustle of people streaming along the dock. Jake glanced at the stalls selling cooked meats, salted fish and wooden cups of steaming cider. His attention was caught by a fortune-teller shrouded in a lace shawl, her wizened hand clutching tarot cards. She held them up to Jake, imploring him to listen to his destiny. He stopped briefly, his eye drawn by the card at the top of the pack: a smiling skeleton in front of a moonlit sea. The fortune-teller's eyes opened ominously, swimming in cloudy grey.

'Let's not get involved,' said Nathan, firmly taking Jake's arm and guiding him on. 'She probably works for the tourist office.'

The three of them skirted round the royal palace, then crossed a wide timber bridge into the formal square in front of the opera house – a graceful three-tiered building capped by a giant stone crown. A steady stream of carriages was arriving, from which the cream of Stockholm's society – all wrapped in furs – disembarked and entered the building.

'Opera?' Nathan complained. 'Is there anything more ridiculous? Overweight people warbling on about nothing! Couldn't that rogue Isaksen have arranged a rendezvous somewhere more appropriate?'

'How dare you, Nathan Wylder! How dare you!' Charlie fumed. 'This is a wonderful performance of Mozart's *The Magic Flute*. It was written only a year ago. The ink is barely dry on the manuscript and the great man is already dead – God rest his soul. It's a once-in-a-lifetime opportunity.'

Nathan pulled a guilty face at Jake and the three of them forged on through the crowds to the entrance.

Meanwhile two figures on horseback emerged

from the shadows on the other side of the square, their gaze fixed on the three agents. They dismounted, and the first, dressed in a high-collared coat, stepped into the half-light of a street lantern. He was tall, upright, and had straight shoulder-length fair hair. His accomplice wore a dark cloak and a distinctive wide-brimmed hat. The blond man whispered something in his companion's ear, gave him charge of his horse, then hurried across the square in pursuit.

Jake's eyes lit up at the sight of the foyer. In contrast to the wintry gloom outside, it was an immense space of white marble and gilded mirrors, lit by constellations of chandeliers. Its inhabitants were as magnificent as the surroundings: poised, elegant people, the polished black boots of the men and the long silk dresses of the ladies reflected in the gleaming floor. Many were arranged in chattering clusters; others were ascending a grand staircase, their eyes eagerly scanning the crowds for the latest source of scandal.

Nathan was in his element. 'I genuinely think this might be one of fashion's all-time greatest moments,' he announced, sweeping off his fur coat to reveal a splendid ultramarine jacket and breeches. 'Look at the silhouettes, look at the detailing, the sheer pizzazz. Their buttons alone could win prizes.'

An attendant wearing a coiffed wig, white gloves and an expression of loathing helped Jake and Charlie out of their coats. Jake's hand caught in his sleeve, and an undignified tussle was followed by the sound of ripping.

'Ooops.' He blushed and tried to stifle a giggle as he passed it to the man. The attendant merely sighed, collected all three overcoats and exchanged them for ivory counters with golden numbers before he withdrew.

'And be careful with my coat,' Nathan called after him. 'It was worn by the Duke of Marlborough at the Battle of Blenheim.' He then confided to Jake, 'Not really, but you can never be too careful with vintage fur.'

A bell sounded and the opera-goers started making their way into the auditorium.

'Well, we might as well get it over with,' Nathan sighed. 'The opera is not going to bore itself. Where are our seats?'

'Royal circle, box M,' Charlie replied curtly, indicating the next tier.

The three of them headed up the stairs, oblivious to the figure with long blond hair, who watched them keenly from behind a pillar.

Another white-gloved attendant led them along a candle-lit corridor and through a door into their private box. It was a small room lined in dark red, with four gilt chairs and a spectacular view of the auditorium. Jake felt another surge of excitement – it was like being inside a giant jewellery case. Five tiers rose up from the stalls in a sweeping oval shape, each containing a succession of private boxes with a batch of gossiping aristocrats. It was like some crazy human zoo – everyone was looking around and whispering slyly to their neighbours.

'Well, where *is* Caspar Isaksen?' asked Nathan with a wry look at the empty chair. 'He's late.' He picked up a pair of silver opera glasses laid out on a side table. 'I suppose, while I am here, I may as well study some Swedish architecture . . .' He started to scan the space with the binoculars – and then stopped. 'Intriguing . . .'

Charlie turned to see that the object of Nathan's attention was a box containing three young ladies, coyly blushing at him from behind their fans.

'Oh, please concentrate,' he sighed. 'This is

work, remember.' He snatched the glasses and passed them to Jake. 'I'm sure *you'll* find something more interesting to look at.'

Jake examined the audience more closely. He half fancied inspecting Nathan's three beauties for himself, but felt it would be rude, so he started at the other end of the tier. He had never seen so much wealth, so many expensive clothes and glittering jewels. Suddenly his binoculars picked out a young girl in a white dress sitting on her own. There was something about her that reminded him of Topaz. He felt a pang as he remembered that dreadful night aboard the *Lindwurm* when she had disappeared, probably for ever, into the vortex of time. To take his mind off the memory, he swiftly continued along the row. Two boxes on, his gaze alighted upon a fair-haired man pointing a silver pistol directly towards him.

Jake gasped, dropped the binoculars, picked them up, looked through them again, shook his head, turned them the right way round and quickly searched for the box once more.

It was empty. The man was nowhere to be seen.

'What on earth is wrong with you?' Nathan asked.

'The box over there! There was a man pointing a gun.'

Nathan and Charlie examined the offending box. An elderly gentleman and his wife were now taking their seats.

'He's gone now, but I promise you I saw him.'

Nathan and Charlie gave each other a look.

'You're new to this' – Nathan meant to be reassuring, but of course it came out as condescending – 'so you're jumpy, that's all. It's the opera; everyone is spying on everyone else. That's the name of the game.'

'He wasn't spying. He was pointing a gun, a silver gun,' Jake insisted.

'Silver?' Nathan noted. 'You're quite sure they weren't opera glasses?'

In truth, Jake wasn't one hundred per cent certain. The moment had been so fleeting.

'Besides, not a soul knows we're here. Only Commander Goethe has our exact time location, so let's not panic.' Nathan leaned over and whispered in Jake's ear, 'If I were you, I'd be more frightened of what's about to happen out there.' He pointed at the stage.

Jake nodded and tried to calm his thumping heart.

An excited hush descended around the theatre as the lights started to fade. A moment later, the orchestra suddenly struck up in a great fanfare of horns and bass drums. Jake once again scanned the tiers of people in search of the blond man, but there were just too many people. Everyone was leaning forward, eyeglasses poised. Another blast of trumpets, and then the violins began.

Jake felt a chill go down his spine as the curtains slowly rose, revealing a dark landscape. At first this was difficult to make out, but a series of lighting effects, each one drawing sighs of admiration from the crowd, gradually illuminated the stage: in the background, a huge moon hung above mountains and pyramids; in the foreground stood palm trees and giant flowers.

'We're in Egypt,' Charlie whispered in awed tones, 'in the realm of the Queen of the Night. In a moment Tamino is going to enter, pursued by a giant serpent.'

'It's a roller coaster,' added Nathan, stifling a yawn.

There was a soft ripple of applause as the young hero materialized out of the desert mist, then fearful

16

sighs as a giant snake curled down from above. At the sight of this, Jake froze. He knew the reptile was nothing but a piece of stage machinery – albeit a very convincing one – but memories quickly came flooding back. It was only a short time ago that he had been thrown into a hideous chamber of snakes and ladders. At the last minute he had been saved by two other History Keepers' agents – his mum and dad, actually – but the incident had left a scar.

Gradually the stage filled with curious characters: three mysterious ladies in veils, a man dressed as a bird – 'Mr Drake would have hooted with laughter,' Charlie commented – then, heralded by ominous claps of thunder, a majestic, fantastical figure took shape out of the stars.

'*That's* the Queen of the Night,' Charlie murmured as she emerged high above the others. 'She's going to ask Tamino to save her daughter from the clutches of the evil sorcerer Sarastro. It seems like she's this frightened mother,' he carried on breathlessly, 'but actually she's the villain and wants to steal the sun and plunge the world into darkness.'

'Don't they all? Mothers-in-law?' Nathan said

with a mischievous smile.

Jake was so hypnotized by this figure, so lost in her spine-tingling voice, so focused on her evil eyes, that when a knock came at the door behind him, he jumped in shock.

He and his companions turned round.

Another knock came, but this time it was followed by three sneezes and then a high voice: 'It's me, Caspar.'

All three of them gave sighs of relief. Nathan opened up and Caspar Isaksen squeezed himself into the box. Jake stared. Caspar was his age, but as wide as he was short, with ruddy cheeks, a runny nose and crazy fair hair going off in all directions. He had a worried smile and glistened with a layer of perspiration. He wore a bright turquoise jacket and breeches that were far too small for him, and Jake noticed that he had done up his buttons wrong.

'Sorry – so sorry I'm late,' Caspar puffed, madly wiping his nose and dabbing his forehead with a handkerchief. 'Hello. Caspar Isaksen . . .' He shook Jake's hand, then Charlie's. 'Ah, Nathan! We've met, of course. As you can see, I didn't forget your advice – you said turquoise would do wonders for my figure. I *never* wear anything else,' he added with

18

great pride, then turned to show off his outfit from all sides and caught sight of the stage for the first time. 'Good heavens! The Queen of the Night is already on! Has she sent Tamino on his mission? She's a sly one, isn't she?'

Nathan was already losing patience. 'Yes, yes – but business first. I take it the atomium's in there?' he asked with a nod towards the holdall in Caspar's hand.

'The atomium is—' Caspar froze mid-sentence, holding up his finger. Jake was just wondering what was going to happen next when suddenly the other boy sneezed. Then again; and a third time for luck.

'Sorry, sorry,' Caspar sighed, wiping his face with his damp handkerchief. 'You're quite right – business first.' He knelt down, opened his case and started to remove the contents. Jake, Nathan and Charlie watched, bewildered, as he unloaded cake after cake after cake. 'I couldn't come to Stockholm without paying a visit to Sundbergs Konditori. Strawberry custard, cinnamon bun, Christmas knäck – yummy yummy,' he muttered as he laid them out one by one.

Finally, from the bottom of the bag, he retrieved a small veneered box. He wiped off a layer of icing sugar and a dollop of cream, and passed it to Nathan. A concentrated stillness descended on the agents. Jake could see that the top of the box was inscribed with an elaborate I – for Isaksen. Nathan opened it, and a golden light shimmered across their faces.

Inside, in a midnight-blue casing, lay two crystal vials, each full to the brim of the infinitely precious liquid.

'That's one consignment for Point Zero,' said Caspar in a more business-like tone, 'and one for the Chinese bureau.'

Nathan was just closing the case when Jake caught sight of a face in the crowd and his stomach churned. Down in the stalls, everyone was looking in the same direction, their faces bathed in light from the stage – except for one person: the blond man seated in the far corner, who was staring fixedly up at them.

'There!' Jake shouted out, pointing at him.

Nathan, Charlie and Caspar turned at once and saw the figure quickly rise from his seat, a silver pistol in his hand. Nathan snatched the opera glasses from Jake and used them to follow the man as he ran up the aisle and stormed through the double doors.

'We've been compromised!' he exclaimed. 'Back to the ship immediately!' He chucked the binoculars back at Jake and carefully took hold of the box of atomium. He adjusted something – Jake couldn't see what – inside, then flung open the door and looked both ways along the curving corridor: nothing but flickering candelabra. 'Charlie, you go that way. Whoever gets to the *Tulip* first, prepare to set sail straight away.'

In a heartbeat, Charlie was racing along the corridor and disappearing down the stairs at the end.

'Jake, Caspar, come with me!' Nathan barked. Caspar was hurriedly picking up his cakes and putting them back in his bag. 'Now!'

Nathan led the way, heading in the opposite direction to Charlie. Jake followed, with Caspar wheezing behind. Footsteps approached from the other end of the passage and a figure appeared.

The three agents froze. Time seemed to stand still as Jake saw their adversary clearly for the first time. He was the same age as Nathan – sixteen or thereabouts – and in many ways a crueller, fair-haired version of him. He had striking features, a superior look in his eye and, judging by his tailored clothes, the same pride in his appearance. His hair, in particular, was a work of art: long, blond and perfectly straight.

Jake could see that Nathan had gone pale.

'Who in God's name is that—' the American started to say as the man raised his pistol – and fired.

2 The Wide-brimmed Hat

The bullet whistled over their heads and struck one of the crystal chandeliers. It came down on the floor behind them with a crash.

'That was a warning shot,' the boy announced silkily in a slight foreign accent. 'You will give me the box,' he said, holding out his hand as he advanced. 'Resistance is pointless. Your sword is no match for my Chaumette flintlock,' he added with a shake of his beautifully crafted gun.

There was a pause, then Nathan spoke calmly. 'All right,' he said, lifting his hands, with the box in clear view. 'I'm not prepared to die over a couple of bottles of *the undrinkable*. You win.'

'Nathan?' Jake exclaimed in disbelief.

'No, I don't think that's such a good idea . . .' Caspar whimpered. He was peering over Jake's shoulder and mopping his brow with his handkerchief.

Nathan ignored them, keeping his attention on the stranger. 'What's your name?' he asked politely. 'I don't believe we've met.'

The blond boy sniggered. 'Impertinent question.' But after a pause, he shrugged and replied, 'You can call me the Leopard.'

'Leopard? Great moniker.'

'*The* Leopard,' the boy snarled with a shake of his perfect fair hair. 'I'm one of a kind.'

'That I can see,' Nathan concurred. 'Your double-breasted waistcoat is *way* ahead of its time, and the Chinese button detailing on your breeches is, frankly, sublime.'

The smile on the Leopard's face faded. 'Just hand over the box.' He levelled his pistol with one hand while holding out the other.

Nathan clenched his jaw, took a deep breath and gave it to him.

Just for a second as he opened the box, the boy took his eye off Nathan – and saw that it was empty. Then everything happened at once. Nathan snatched Caspar's sodden handkerchief and threw it into the Leopard's face, where it stuck, blinding him completely. The gun went off, but the bullet went through the ceiling. Nathan kicked high and smashed his boot into his opponent's jaw. The boy teetered backwards, lost his balance completely and landed in a tangle on the floor, his head giving a *crack* as it hit the wall.

'I lied – those Chinese buttons are the height of vulgarity,' Nathan said as he and the others escaped down the corridor. At the far end, he threw open the door to another box and quickly pushed Jake and Caspar inside. He bolted the entrance behind them and turned to face the occupants. It was the three pretty ladies he had spied earlier.

They stood in shock, clutching the jewels around their necks, but clearly relishing the intrusion. 'Under different circumstances' – Nathan tossed his auburn locks and showed his glinting teeth – 'this might have been hello and not goodbye . . . Quickly, you two,' he said, throwing his legs over the balcony and jumping down into the stalls, provoking murmurs of annoyance amongst the audience. As he hit the carpet, the bottles of atomium slipped out of his pocket. He quickly scooped them up.

Jake nodded politely at the girls, while Caspar

froze, turning crimson and clutching his bag of cakes to his chest. As Jake helped him to clamber over the balustrade, the unfortunate girls were treated to the sight of his bright turquoise trousers ripping – revealing a half-moon of large pink back-side. They tore even more as Caspar awkwardly scrambled his way to the floor – giving the whole audience a glimpse of his derrière. Jake followed with a single athletic vault. As he landed, Nathan pressed the two bottles of atomium into Jake's hand. 'Holes in my pockets,' he said, patting his jacket. 'You hold onto them.'

Jake felt a sudden flutter of panic, of daunting responsibility, but he slipped them into the deep pouches inside his jacket.

'This way,' Nathan commanded, skirting round the auditorium to the exit at the back. He stopped dead when he saw the Leopard swing through the doors, then turned on his heel and cut straight along a row of seats. The others followed, apologizing as they pushed their way past the acres of fine silk and crinoline. Caspar yanked up his trousers, tripping over their priceless shoes and shedding chunks of Christmas knäck as he did so, provoking jeers of outrage; one ancient lady was so furious, she bashed him over the head with her fan.

'Quickly, quickly.' Jake pushed him into the aisle. The Leopard was now bearing swiftly down on them and they had no choice but to run up the steps at the front of the auditorium. A great swathe of opera-goers half stood in astonishment as the three of them shuffled over the bridge spanning the orchestra pit and onto the stage itself. The Queen of the Night did not falter in her aria; rather she focused her falsetto fury on the invaders, hurling notes at them like barbed daggers.

The Leopard quickened his pace and was on the point of firing his pistol again when a number of guards – they'd evidently been alerted to an incident – quickly filed in through the side doors, muskets at the ready. The Leopard froze and slowly replaced his weapon in its holster. Realizing that it would be madness to try anything now, he reluctantly slunk back up the aisle.

Nathan watched him retreat before turning roguishly towards the Queen of the Night. 'Love your work – simply spine-tingling . . .' He saluted her with a theatrical air-kiss. 'Mortified to be missing the denouement.' The rest of the cast watched, slack-jawed, as the three agents steered their way around the set – with Caspar bumping into a pyramid and toppling a palm tree – and exited into the wings.

They flew along the backstage passageways, weaving their way through clusters of performers, set-movers, candle men and wig-makers. They tore down stairs into a strange underworld of old props and painted backdrops; slithers of history piled up against each other. Jake noticed one in particular: a vast rendition of the Colosseum of ancient Rome – a gigantic crumbling arena beneath a bold blue sky. For a second he lost himself in it before Nathan pushed him on along the network of passages.

By the time the three of them reached a side exit – one of many leading out of the opera house – Caspar looked half dead, his chest heaving like a bellows. Nathan carefully edged open the door and checked that the coast was clear. There was a line of carriages parked along the side of the building and a huddle of drivers playing cards, rubbing their hands together to keep warm.

Nathan signalled to the others, and they crept out and ducked down in the shadows behind the coaches. From here they could see the main entrance. At length, the Leopard marched out –

darting his head this way and that in search of his prey. He quickly strode over to his accomplice, a man in a wide-brimmed hat, and spoke to him. The latter then mounted his horse and disappeared round the far side of the building.

Nathan motioned for Caspar and Jake to climb into one of the carriages. Jake carefully opened the gilt-framed door and let himself into the silky interior. When Caspar stepped up, the whole vehicle creaked under his weight, sinking down on one side. As the card players looked round to see what the noise was Nathan jumped up onto the driver's seat and flicked the reins.

The horses didn't move.

The drivers started shouting and ran towards him – immediately alerting the Leopard to what was going on – and he flicked the reins again. 'Come on, come on!' Nathan begged. When he finally stood up and delivered a sharp kick to each rump, they suddenly whinnied and took off, careering across the square.

In a flash the Leopard mounted his steed and whistled for his companion. The man in the wide-brimmed hat came charging back and they tore off in pursuit of the carriage. Two of the other carriage drivers, outraged at the theft, leaped up onto their own vehicles and joined the chase. The convoy hurtled across the bridge, with Nathan at its head.

Jake and Caspar were shaken violently as the wheels juddered over the wooden planks. Then they were hurled to one side as the coach swerved round a corner, Jake crushed under Caspar's huge belly. Once they had righted themselves again, the Swede, his hands trembling, fished some broken pieces of knäck out of his bag and starting shovelling them into his mouth.

'What are you doing?' Jake shook his head in disbelief.

'Sugar calms me down in an emergency,' Caspar spluttered, scooping up another handful.

Suddenly a gunshot rang out and a bullet smashed through the window behind them. Jake glanced back – a biting wind now blowing in his face – and saw the Leopard tearing up the hill, a smoking pistol in his hand, with his partner galloping swiftly behind.

Suddenly the carriage veered to one side again as Nathan swung round another bend, the wheels skidding on the ice. He shook the reins again, weaving skilfully through the narrow cobbled streets of the old town – up, down, left and right – as their pursuers tried to catch them.

The two vehicles at the back did not make it: the leading one tried to navigate a sharp bend but it met a patch of black ice and skidded across the road, smashing, in a shower of sparks, into the steps of a church, completely blocking the path of the second.

Nathan plunged down the hill towards the harbour. Between the narrow buildings, far below on the dockside, he could see the hulking silhouette of the warship, next to which the *Tulip* was berthed. Then disaster struck. A cart laden with coal came tottering over a crossroads ahead, blocking his way. The horses reared up, whinnying, their hooves slipping on the ice. Suddenly the whole carriage swung round and took charge of its own destiny. With an ear-splitting screech, it crashed into the window of a cake shop, plunging into an elaborate display of baked goods.

Nathan dismounted in a flash and pulled open the door for the others. 'Quickly! Quickly!' he yelled, helping them out.

'Sundbergs Konditori!' Caspar suddenly gasped on seeing the name of shop they had just crashed into. He quivered at the sight of a thousand buns and cakes ready for the taking; but Nathan and Jake took an arm each and dragged him down a steep flight of steps to the port. Within seconds they were lost in a labyrinth of narrow passageways and winding steps which the others, on their horses, could not negotiate.

They came to a wide portico that led, through a series of arches, into the customs house – a great high-windowed chamber still full of activity and chattering people even though it was well into the evening. Throngs of richly dressed merchants haggled with dour, bespectacled officials as goods were weighed, and gold and silver coins counted and reluctantly handed over. Nathan, Jake and Caspar weaved their way through the busy crowd (amongst the exotic-looking people here – seafarers from all over the world – even Caspar in his ripped turquoise suit didn't look out of place) to the main door on the other side, which led directly onto the harbour.

'There – look.' Jake pointed at the *Tulip*, further along the dock in the shadow of the warship. He remembered he still had the opera glasses in his trouser pocket. He took them out, surveyed the ship and spotted a figure hoisting the mainsail. 'It's Charlie – he made it.'

But Nathan had seen something else: two riders coming onto the quayside, one fair-haired, the other in a wide-brimmed hat. 'In here – quickly!' he said, darting across the flagstones and up into the fish market.

They were hit immediately by the salty stench of fresh fish. Like the customs house, the market – lit by wax lanterns hanging from the rafters – was bustling with activity. Dock workers were delivering and taking away boxes of fish, while fishermen bartered noisily, their mouths firing gusts of vapour. The agents threaded their way through and hid in the shadows behind three vast stacks of boxes. Caspar pulled a face when he caught sight of their contents: live eels, thrashing and writhing about. Jake and Nathan peered out. Through the throng they saw the Leopard and his sidekick dismount and cautiously approach the other side of the market.

As they came into the light beside the building, the accomplice nudged up his hat to wipe his brow and his face became visible for the first time. Jake started. It was hard to see through the clouds of icy vapour, but he recognized something about him.

He squinted to get a better view and could see that he was young – seventeen or so – handsome, broad shouldered, with olive skin.

Then it dawned on him: his eyes widened and his heart stopped. His hands shook. His face went pale.

'Philip . . . ?' he said softly to himself. The man, he was certain, was his lost brother.

Three years ago, tragedy had come to the Djones family when Philip, Jake's older brother, disappeared, presumed dead. Jake had always been led to believe that the disaster happened on a school trip, and had learned only recently that Philip had actually been on a History Keepers' mission at the time – an assignment to Vienna in 1689. They hadn't heard from him since – but neither had a body been found, and Jake, who had loved his brother deeply, now clung to the belief that he was still alive somewhere.

The phantom said something to the Leopard and they both turned away from the market and headed back to remount their horses. They trotted off along the quay in the other direction, eyes searching for their prey.

'Right, let's go,' Nathan whispered, stepping carefully out from their hiding place. Caspar followed, but Jake paid no attention; he was spellbound, rooted to the spot, watching the two figures retreat. His heart was pumping at double speed, his breaths short and quick, his brain teeming with questions: was that really his brother? It was three years since he had seen him. He had only caught a fleeting glance – but is that what he would look like now? And if it *was* his brother, why was he here with the enemy? Jake wanted to cry out '*Philip?*' at the top of his voice and see if he turned round.

'What in God's name are you doing!' Nathan hissed, coming back and taking Jake's arm. 'Let's go!' He dragged him through the market and onto the quayside towards the *Tulip*. Half in a dream, Jake turned again. The two riders were almost out of sight. He stared at the figure in the wide-brimmed hat.

'Nathan, I know you're going to think I'm crazy,' he said, finally stopping and turning, 'but I cannot leave here until I know something.' He started wandering, as if in a trance, towards the riders.

Jake was right: Nathan *did* think he was mad. 'Come back here!' he thundered. 'Come back at once!'

The horsemen, hearing the voices, stopped and

turned. They peered into the half-light and made out the silhouettes behind them on the quay – and started heading back.

'We have precisely a minute to get out of here.' Nathan yanked Jake on across the icy cobbles towards the *Tulip*, Caspar panting at his side.

'Here!' Charlie identified himself from the prow. 'Furnace lit, ready to set sail.' All the History Keepers' vessels, whatever age they originally came from, were modified for speed, and the *Tulip*'s propeller was turning slowly in the water.

They were just ten yards away when Jake, unable to contain his curiosity any longer, twisted free of Nathan and turned towards the two riders, who were now fast approaching along the quay.

'Philip?' he shouted at the top of his voice. 'Is it you?'

'Stop it!' Nathan yelled, once again taking hold of Jake.

'Let go of me!' Jake snarled, swinging his arm savagely and cracking his fist into Nathan's jaw. Charlie, who was not prone to dramatic gestures, held up his hands and gasped in horror.

'He has the atomium!' Nathan said as Jake ran back along the quay towards the horsemen. He froze, unable to process what he should do next.

'Philip, is it you?' Jake called again, half demented. He stopped as the Leopard's horse drew up at his side, its rider cocking his pistol and pointing it at him. Jake paid no heed to it. He wasn't scared; all he cared about was the identity of the other man.

This figure now approached and, in an instant, jumped down from his horse. He advanced slowly towards Jake, his face still in shadow. Jake could feel tears welling up. 'Philip . . .?' he asked in a desperate, quavering voice.

For the first time, the man removed his hat.

Immediately the hope drained from Jake. Close up, he could see, with terrible clarity, that this was *not* his brother: wrong nose, wrong mouth, wrong eyes. It was a complete stranger. Now the impostor also drew his weapon and, with a sly smile, aimed it at Jake.

'We'll take those vials now,' the Leopard said in his silky voice. 'Henrik, would you oblige?'

Henrik jabbed his gun closer towards Jake's chest.

Nathan, Charlie and Caspar could only watch powerlessly as Jake retrieved the two bottles from inside his jacket and passed them over. Henrik in turn handed them to the Leopard, who slotted them back into their original box. 'Such a pleasure doing business.' He bowed to the forlorn agents of the History Keepers as Henrik replaced his hat and mounted his horse.

Suddenly a cry came out of nowhere: 'Noooooooo!' Caspar screamed as he rushed towards the Leopard. 'It doesn't belong to you!' Then there was an explosion – a gun was discharged so close it made Jake's ears pop. Smoke was coming from the Leopard's pistol. For a moment no one moved, then Caspar gasped in agony, his eyes swimming in shock. Blood seeped through his fingers as he clutched his abdomen. He slipped on the ice, lost his balance and fell into the sea.

'Caspar!' Jake shouted. He was about to launch himself into the harbour when he noticed Henrik's gun trained on him once again.

'Do we kill them?' Henrik asked.

But the Leopard had noticed activity on the deck of the warship docked next to the *Tulip*. A group of soldiers had spotted the fight and were disembarking, heading towards them.

'Too late,' he said decisively. 'We have what we

need.' The two of them turned their horses round and charged off.

'Caspar!' Jake shouted again, now tearing over to the quayside. He was about to throw himself into the water when Nathan yanked him back.

'Stay there!' he said furiously. 'You've caused enough damage!'

Jake watched, his lips quivering, his face ashen, as Nathan dived into the freezing sea, yelling at the shock that immediately made his lungs seize up. When he reached Caspar, the boy was wheezing and trying to move his arms, but his body was stiff, motionless, already frozen. On the other side of the harbour Jake could see the Leopard and his sidekick – the man who might have been his brother – heading up a narrow alley and out of sight.

Charlie ran to Jake's side, ready to help the others out of the water. 'I'd say they have about a minute before their vital organs start closing down,' he murmured.

Nathan managed to drag Caspar back to the quayside, where Jake and Charlie started to haul him up. This was an almost impossible task: he was unconscious and seemed to weigh more than the two of them put together. They made four unsuccessful attempts before a group of Swedish soldiers from the warship came to help. Finally they were laying him out on the stones. For a second Jake, Nathan and Charlie stood over his prone body, chests heaving, teeth chattering. The soldiers stood wide-eyed at their side.

Nathan sank to his knees, put his hands on Caspar's chest and started to push down repeatedly, stopping every so often to blow air into his mouth. For a while the boy remained motionless. Jake bit his lip in anxiety. Finally Caspar vomited seawater, gasped and opened his eyes. He was conscious, but only barely so.

Nathan immediately turned his attention to the gunshot wound. He could see the entry point to the left of Caspar's abdomen, and could feel an exit hole round the back. The blood that had congealed in the freezing water was now starting to seep out again. He turned to the soldiers. 'On board?' he asked. 'Do you have a hospital? *Har ni ett sjukhus?*'

The soldiers nodded, then picked up Caspar and carried him towards the warship.

The unfortunate Swede was laid out on an operating table in the cramped, low-ceilinged cabin that was the ship's sickbay. His face was white, his jaw shaking, and he was mumbling to himself feverishly. A masked surgeon, eyes red from tiredness, was threading a needle by the light of an oil lantern. Nathan and Charlie stood watching; Jake waited sheepishly by the doorway. On the wall behind the operating table he eyed up a collection of instruments – ancient medical tools, blades and eye-watering saws, some black with dried blood.

The doctor uttered something in Swedish.

'This is going to sting a bit,' Charlie translated quietly. He nodded at Nathan and they each held one of the patient's arms, while a soldier grabbed his legs.

Caspar yelled out loud and thrashed about as the surgeon inserted the needle. Jake winced and had to clench his jaw. Eight gruelling minutes passed (it seemed more like an hour) before the thread was finally tied and the wound cleaned and dressed.

Eventually Caspar's delirium passed and his breathing steadied. As he came to his senses, he realized he was angry. His eyes sought out Jake's; they seemed to burn like embers as they stared savagely at him. 'You . . .' he spat. 'I wish to say something to you.'

41

Jake nodded and stepped forward. 'I'm so, so sorry,' he sighed softly. 'It's my fault that you were shot.'

'Shot?' Caspar spat. 'Do you think I care about that? It's nothing compared to the damage *you* have done.'

Jake could only hang his head and take his punishment. Caspar was no longer merely the clumsy, amusing boy who liked cakes and opera. He continued through gritted teeth: 'I don't know who you are, or where you've come from, or what you have to do with the History Keepers' Secret Service, but you need to know that you have ruined everything. *Everything.* It is not just that it took ten years to distil that atomium; or that it will take another ten to replace it; or that vital, life-saving missions may now have to be aborted because of your folly. No, worse than all this, you have armed our enemies – armed them with the power to take control of history like never before. So, whatever your name is – I neither remember nor care – feel bad . . . *feel like a traitor – because that's what you are.*'

Jake gulped and a tear rolled down his cheek.

3 JOSEPHINE OF NANTES

'Where on earth did she get them?' Miriam asked under her breath.

'From a circus ringmaster in Nantes, she told me,' Alan whispered back. 'He'd fallen on hard times and had to sell off his animals to pay his debts. Apparently Oceane only wanted one of them – she'd fallen in love *à première vue* – but was forced to take the whole lot as part of the deal.'

It was an exceptionally blustery day on the Mont St Michel. Alan and Miriam, Jake's mum and dad, were standing on the pier, along with a collection of similarly intrigued History Keepers, as Oceane Noire, bossing everyone around in her usual haughty manner, oversaw the arrival of her 'menagerie' of circus animals. Everyone was dressed, Miriam and Alan included, in clothes of the 1820s, the women in long gowns and the men in tailcoats, breeches and top hats. There was a sudden gust of wind and the ladies' dresses flapped violently, while the men clung onto their top hats.

A barge had docked and the crew were guiding various bemused-looking beasts down the gangplank onto the quay: a pair of ponies and a couple of horses were followed – quite dramatically – by a lumbering elephant. All the animals were a little past their prime, but the elephant looked very ancient and tired, its back sagging, its head drooping, its skin rough and worn.

'Poor thing,' Miriam sighed. There was such a sad look in its eye, it brought a tear to her own. Alan put his arm round her and gave her a cuddle.

Needless to say, Oceane was not moved; in fact, she could barely hide her disgust. She sprinkled a few drops of perfume onto a silk handkerchief and held it to her nose as the beast shambled past. When it stopped, turned and swung its trunk in her direction, she shrieked out loud and threw herself into the arms of Jupitus Cole, who was also staring, with typically icy blankness, at the bizarre scene.

To the bafflement of everyone at Point Zero – the tiny Mont St Michel in Normandy – Jupitus and

Oceane had recently announced their engagement. He was the dour Victorian second-in-command, she a tricky heiress from the court of Louis XV. And though they were in every way as haughty as each other, no one had ever guessed at romance between them.

'Where on earth is she going to put them?' Miriam asked her husband.

'Galliana has said they can go in the old stable block for the time being,' Alan replied, 'but she is not impressed!'

Miriam looked at the commander. On the surface she seemed as calm as ever, but she was clearly displeased.

'We're supposed to be a secret service,' Galliana muttered, 'not drawing attention to ourselves with circus animals . . . though they do look like a friendly lot.'

'Just as well,' said Miriam with a mischievous smile, 'as you'll probably be cleaning up after them. Somehow I can't quite see Oceane Noire sweeping up elephant dung.'

At this moment, as if to demonstrate her point, the elephant lifted its tail and posted a package from its behind. Two great lumps of grassy brown compost landed on the ground with a thud.

'*Oh, mon dieu, mon dieu!*' Oceane gasped, clutching the pearls around her neck as if the animal had delivered a couple of live bombs.

'Told you,' Miriam commented. 'She's never seen one of those before. Of course, she doesn't produce any herself.'

She and Alan looked at each other; in unison their eyes flashed, their lips trembled and they started giggling.

The final animal to emerge from the cargo hold, the chains around her neck held very firmly and warily by two members of the crew, was a young lioness. There was a collective intake of breath as she padded onto the quayside. She was little more than a cub, not yet grown into her giant paws, but already had a sly look in her eye.

'There she is!' Oceane exclaimed, running towards the creature. '*Ma petite.*' There were more gasps as she knelt down and actually threw her arms around the lioness. 'We don't need these silly shackles,' she said, unfastening the chains and tossing them at the two crewmen. 'Josephine is quite tame; she was reared by humans – by French blue bloods, no less . . . the ringmaster was a distant relation of Eleanor of Aquitaine. Look, she even eats rocket.' Oceane snapped her fingers at one of her browbeaten attendants, who duly handed her an embroidered bag. From this she produced a handful of leaves and held them out. The lioness sniffed them a couple of times, then consumed them without a great deal of interest.

'Isn't she the cleverest thing?' Oceane trilled, clapping her hands together in excitement. *'Adorable, tout simplement!* And don't you love the name? Just like Madame Bonaparte herself.'

There was another gust of wind – this one strong enough to sweep up Alan's hat and carry it off, first in a swirling eddy around the mount, and then out to sea. He and Miriam watched as it dropped into the rolling waves.

'Wasn't keen on it anyway,' Alan announced with a shrug. 'Signor Gondolfino said it would "set off" my face, but it just made my head itch.' Miriam started giggling again, and he joined in.

'Take all the other beasts to the stables,' Oceane ordered her flunky, then turned to her young lioness. 'Come on, my darling, let's get you inside, *il fait trop de vent.*' She led the beast by the scruff towards the main doors of the castle. 'I'm going to find you something clever to wear around your neck. I'm feeling diamonds – how about you?'

The lioness stopped and gazed with narrowed eyes at the assembled company, then they both went inside.

As Oceane's attendant guided the elephant and the other animals to the stables, Miriam looked out towards the horizon. 'Jake should be back soon. I do hope everything went all right.'

Since they had set sail from Stockholm across the thawing sea, the mood aboard the *Tulip* had been solemn.

Before they left, Nathan and Charlie had transported Caspar to the house of a family friend (Jake had not been allowed to accompany them, but instructed to wait alone below deck), and had sent word to the Isaksens to collect him. They had bought some provisions for the return journey and set off as the sun started to rise over the sea. It had turned out to be the first warm day in weeks and the ice had begun to melt instantly.

For hours Jake had skulked in the background, offering to assist wherever he could – to help Nathan unfurl the sails or lend Charlie a hand in the galley. Both had declined his offers with a terse shake of the head, barely looking at him. Mr Drake had also seemed to pick up on the atmosphere. Jake had offered him some of the fruitcake that his mum had pressed into his hand on his departure. Though the parrot usually loved cake (even Miriam's disastrously tipsy concoction), he had declined it with a toss of his head and had flown off to perch on the yardarm. That was when Jake had retreated to his cabin.

As it started to get dark again, Jake was still picking over the awful events in Stockholm. *Feel like a traitor – because that's what you are*, Caspar Isaksen had told him bluntly. The knowledge that he had let people down – not just his new friends, but *all* the History Keepers – was bad enough; but the notion that his actions might lead directly to the suffering of innocent people was so dreadful it turned his stomach to liquid.

Charlie knocked on the cabin door and asked if he would like some polenta and porcini fricassee. Although Jake didn't have a clue what it was, he accepted with exaggerated enthusiasm.

Over dinner he kept respectfully silent as Nathan and Charlie discussed who the Leopard might be working for and how he'd come by the precise details of the keepers' rendezvous with Caspar Isaksen at the Stockholm opera house.

'I hate to be the voice of doom,' Nathan said, putting his empty plate to one side and retrieving a small veneered box, 'but what other explanation can there be?' He opened the box and took out its contents: the silver Horizon Cup and two small vials of liquid – the remaining atomium for their return journey to Point Zero. He set the destination dial on the silver device and muttered grimly, 'There must be another double agent amongst us.' It had been a matter of weeks since Norland, the seemingly amiable chauffeur, had been uncovered as a spy at Point Zero.

The three agents drank their doses of vile liquid, Charlie sharing a few drops with a reluctant Mr Drake, and an hour later they hit the horizon point. Here Jake experienced the usual out-of-body sensations, accompanied by the same flashing snapshots of history in his mind's eye; but partly because of the short distance they were travelling – just twenty-eight years – and partly because of his lingering feeling of guilt, the ride wasn't as thrilling as it had been before.

Soon after arriving in the less chilly waters of 1820, the *Tulip*'s engines suddenly stalled. Nathan stripped off his shirt ('Oil and Japanese silk are a match made in hell,' he explained) and tried to repair a ruptured gasket. In the end, however, he and Charlie were worried about the risk of fire and decided to continue using wind power alone. It was past one in the morning when Charlie finally spied the distinctive conical silhouette of the Mont St Michel in the distance, and almost two by the time they drifted across the bay.

'It looks like Galliana's waited up for us,' said Charlie, nodding towards the light in a casement window high up in the castle.

Jake's heart thumped a little harder as the island, its flanks covered in building upon building, loomed up ahead of him: he had been hoping, as they were arriving so late, that the news of his 'treachery' might wait until morning. That was evidently not to be. He searched the black façade for more lights, particularly in the tower where his mum and dad slept. It saddened him a little to discover that this part of the building was pitch-black; they must have already gone to bed.

'Jake,' Charlie called across to him. 'Nathan and

I have discussed everything: when we arrive, let *us* do the talking. There's no point in you getting into unnecessary trouble.'

'I don't think I would feel right about that,' Jake replied in a quiet voice. 'I'm to blame.'

'Blame is pointless,' Charlie persisted. 'It doesn't get anyone anywhere. We'll sort it out, all right?'

Jake still felt unsure about this but he reluctantly agreed. 'Thank you.'

Charlie shrugged. 'That's what friends are for. We all make mistakes. It's how you learn from them that's important.'

Jake appreciated Charlie saying this, but as he watched Nathan, sullenly coiling ropes at the prow of the ship, he wondered whether the American's forgiveness would be a little harder to earn.

'There he is! There's our boy,' a familiar voice called out from the shadows as they drew in to the quayside.

Jake searched the darkness to find two figures reclining on sun loungers, wrapped up in blankets.

'Mum? Dad?' he exclaimed joyfully, temporarily forgetting his troubles. He leaped down onto the pier. 'What are you doing here?'

'What are we doing here, Miriam?' Alan turned to his wife. 'Taking the pleasant night air, aren't we?' he said, referring to the blustery wind. 'We're waiting for you, you daft plank.'

Miriam stood up and threw her arms around her son. 'How are you, darling? Good trip?'

Jake tried to nod, but it came out more like a shrug.

'Fancy a nice cup of tea?' Alan asked, giving his son a great bear hug. Jake tried to keep hold of his emotions.

There was a clattering sound, and a shape bounded across the cobbles.

'Felson!' Jake cried as the dog leaped up at him, panting with delight. 'I missed you too,' he said, kneeling so that Felson could give his face a good licking. This was the sturdy, battle-scarred mastiff that had once belonged to his enemy, Captain Von Bliecke. Jake had befriended him when they had both been abandoned at sea.

'He had a nice time with us,' Miriam commented. 'Though of course your father overfed him and let him sleep on the bed – but he never stopped staring at the horizon, waiting for you to come back.'

'So how did our son get on, Mr Chieverley?' Alan asked Charlie as he jumped down from the *Tulip*. 'Did he do us proud?'

'He acquitted himself quite professionally, yes,' Charlie replied in a very business-like voice.

'Blimey,' Alan chuckled. 'That bad, eh?' and he and Miriam started laughing. 'Come on – let's get you all inside.'

The six of them, Jake and his parents, Nathan and Charlie – along with Felson, glued to his master's side – made their way up the steps and through the large double doors into the castle. The wind whistled round the great staircase, making the tapers flicker.

Jake could bear the suspense no longer. 'Mum, Dad, I've got something to tell you—'

'There's Commander Goethe and Jupitus Cole!' Charlie interrupted, and gave Jake a sidelong glance to remind him that *he* was doing the talking.

Galliana and Jupitus were coming down the stairs to meet them. The commander, smiling serenely, was in her dressing gown, and her long silver hair was swept right back. Jupitus, dressed impeccably in a tight-fitting jacket with a starched collar, stepped down in her wake.

As they met halfway, the whole company came to a standstill. Felson looked eagerly from one face to another.

Nathan nodded at Charlie, who spoke first. 'Commander Goethe, Mr Cole, I'm afraid we have bad news.' Jupitus looked up. 'We have failed in our mission. We were intercepted and the entire atomium consignment has been lost.'

'What?' Jupitus gasped in disbelief. 'Lost?'

'Regrettably, yes,' Charlie replied stoically.

'*Regrettably?!* Have you any idea what this means?' Jupitus was livid. 'Who intercepted you?'

'There was a young gentleman who called himself the Leopard,' Charlie went on. 'I intend to start research immediately to find out where he has come from and who he may be working for.'

'But how did this happen?' Jupitus persisted.

'It happened because I mucked everything up,' Jake blurted out. 'I disobeyed orders, completely. Everything was my fault.' Galliana listened carefully while Jupitus's mouth gaped open. 'And I'm afraid that is not all,' Jake continued grimly. 'As a result of my error, Caspar Isaksen was shot.'

'*Shot?*' Jupitus repeated.

Charlie quickly butted in, 'Though it seems he'll make a full recovery.'

Miriam, aware of her son's deep remorse, held him firmly by the shoulders. 'You poor thing . . .' she whispered in his ear.

'Poor thing?' Jupitus scoffed, using the wall to support him in his shock. 'This is a disaster, an unmitigated disaster.'

'Mr Cole, Commander . . .' Nathan finally spoke. 'It was very honourable of Jake to own up, but I can assure you the fault lies with myself more than anyone else. Jake tried to warn me that he had seen a man with a gun, and I did not pay attention. I am the one who was culpable.'

'How civil of you. Such a martyr.' Jupitus shook his head, not believing a word of it.

Despite his distress, Jake felt a warm pulse of happiness: Nathan was his friend after all. There was a degree of truth in what he had said, but Jake knew that he alone was responsible.

Suddenly, at the foot of the stairs, the double doors flew open and the wind gusted in, blowing out the tapers and leaving everyone in almost complete darkness. Alan went down, closed the door and bolted it.

Galliana glanced at Jake, taking the measure of him with her calm grey eyes, before ordering the group, 'Sleep now. We can discuss this further in the morning.'

With heavy hearts everyone made their way up to their beds.

Jake lingered behind for a moment. On the walls, the life-size portraits of famous History Keepers of the past stared at him silently. He turned and looked at one in particular: Sejanus Poppoloe, the founder of the secret service, dressed in his characteristic cloak and turban. His gaze was stern, as if he too understood the magnitude of Jake's treachery.

4 MESLITH FROM DEEP HISTORY

Jake was woken by a commotion in the corridor –
people rushing by, speaking in urgent whispers.
Felson, who was stretched out diagonally across the
bed, also stirred, lifting his head and pricking up his
ears. Jake looked at his clock: it was six thirty in the
morning. Early morning light was peeking through
the curtains. He had been given a room in one of
the oldest parts of the castle. It had ancient casement windows, a small four-poster bed and a
fireplace, where embers still glowed from the night
before.

He got out of bed and put his head round the
door. Jupitus Cole flew by, followed by Truman
Wylder, Nathan's father, buttoning up his shirt as he
hurried down the stairs. Then Signor Gondolfino,
impeccably dressed even at this time of day, limped

by as quickly as his old legs and ivory cane would allow him.

'Has something happened?' Jake asked. He dreaded the answer – maybe some calamity had already taken place as a result of the disaster in Stockholm. But Gondolfino had an entirely new revelation, a piece of news that made Jake's heart beat even faster.

'They think a Meslith has arrived . . . from Topaz St Honoré. Commander Goethe has called an emergency meeting.' A Meslith – Jake was now familiar with the term – was a message that was transmitted through time, sent and received on a Meslith machine, an intriguing typewriter-like instrument with crystalline rods that fizzed with electricity.

Jake dressed at breakneck speed, throwing on his trousers, shirt and jacket. He couldn't find any socks, so he pulled on his boots without them and stuffed the laces inside. 'I'll come back for you in a minute,' he told Felson, and ran out of the room. He tore through the maze of corridors and staircases – sometimes jumping down entire flights – until he arrived at the double doors to the stateroom. He ran his hand through his hair, pulled his collar straight and stepped inside.

Fifteen or so people, mostly older History Keepers, were chatting seriously, some seated around the large table, some gathered in clusters about the room. Light was streaming through the four giant windows that looked out across the sea. Jake immediately felt the hostile gaze of Jupitus Cole, who was seated at the far end of the table with a bundle of maps laid out in front of him. Jake nodded at him and tried to smile. Jupitus merely stared icily back as Jake edged round the room towards Charlie, who was standing next to a buffet table laden with French pastries.

'Do we know anything yet?' asked Jake breathlessly. 'Where did this message come from?'

Charlie held up his hand to indicate that his mouth was full. He carried on munching for a while. 'I always thought brioches were overrated,' he said after he had swallowed the last mouthful, 'but this one has a subtle hint of lemon, which really lifts it. If you're referring to Topaz, I'm as much in the dark as you.' He changed the subject. 'I don't think you've met Dr Chatterju?' he said, indicating a distinctive-looking man in a turban and round spectacles. 'He's in charge of our inventions division. He arrived back from Bombay yesterday . . .'

'A necessary but exhausting trip to see my relations,' Chatterju explained, his voice as elegant as his appearance, 'who are spread, disobligingly, not only throughout India, but throughout the centuries!' He smiled broadly and held out his hand to Jake. 'Zal Chatterju – it's such an honour to meet you. I knew your brother. A wonderful young man. And I sense that you are gifted like him . . . ?'

Jake smiled shyly. He was immediately taken by Chatterju, aware of an eccentric, mischievous mind. The man wore a thickly embroidered kaftan fastened with an ornate golden belt. The face above the perfectly groomed grey beard was distinguished, aristocratic. His turban was secured with a brilliant sapphire that matched his eyes.

'What exactly is the inventions division?' asked Jake.

'Oh, you'll find out soon enough,' Chatterju chuckled. 'I'm just a lowly scientist with a few crackpot ideas.' Suddenly he looked agitated. 'Where has that boy got to? Has he disappeared off again? He's always disappearing!'

'I'm here, Uncle, right behind you.' A young boy stepped out.

'Right behind me? Don't be so impudent. Come here where I can see you.'

The boy did as he was told. He was about eleven, Jake guessed, with a face as warm as dark honey that looked as if it never stopped smiling.

'I'm Amrit,' he introduced himself cheerfully to Jake. 'Dr Chatterju's nephew.'

'My assistant!' Chatterju corrected him. 'That's what you are. And you're very much on trial.' With a roll of the eyes he confided to Jake, 'He's little more than a child but thinks he knows *everything*.'

There was a final influx of people into the room, including Jake's mum, his dad – who was still half asleep and couldn't stop yawning – and his aunt Rose. Behind them trotted Galliana's greyhound, Olive, who immediately padded over to her place at the top of the table. A hush then descended as Galliana herself swept in and took her seat. Jake noticed that she was wearing her long navy cloak embroidered with motifs of clocks and phoenixes, and was holding a bundle of papers.

'Is everyone present?' she asked Jupitus.

'All except Nathan Wylder and Oceane Noire. The former,' Jupitus sighed, 'is apparently working off his frustration with some deep-sea fishing. Mademoiselle Noire is still dressing.'

'So we won't see her until the end of the century,' Miriam chuckled to her husband.

'We'll have to start without them.' Galliana spoke in a quick, business-like voice, looking around at all the faces. 'We have two matters on the agenda: firstly, for those of you who are not up to speed, the mission to Stockholm was unsuccessful. The agents were intercepted by an enemy faction and the atomium consignment was lost.'

There was immediate uproar amongst those gathered, with shouts of:

'*The whole consignment?*'

'*How can that be?*'

'*Who was responsible?*'

Jake shifted uncomfortably, aware of Jupitus's narrowed eyes settling on him once again.

Galliana held up her hand. 'The whys and wherefores of how this happened are irrelevant.' She read from her notes: '*The perpetrator was in his late teens, five feet ten, blond Caucasian. He went by the name of the Leopard. Assisted by a dark-haired youth of a similar age.*' Jake looked down. 'Does this ring any bells?' Galliana asked the group.

Nothing but blank faces. 'Miss Wunderbar . . . ?'

The stately woman in charge of the Library of Faces, beautifully dressed in the fashion of the 1690s, shook her head. 'Nothing, I'm afraid,' she announced in her curt Bavarian accent. 'I'm in the process of a more detailed search of faces. Agent Chieverley is helping me.'

'It goes without saying,' Galliana continued, 'that *anyone* who can shed any light on the matter should come forward immediately. This is of paramount importance. Now, to the second matter . . .' She withdrew a piece of parchment from her bundle. 'I received this message an hour ago, apparently sent from deep history.'

Jake craned his neck to see: he could just make out a very long series of symbols.

'Obviously it was encoded in Hypoteca, which has been translated as follows.' Galliana held up another scroll for all to see. This one contained more numbers, in larger, bolder type.

'What's Hypoteca?' Jake whispered to Charlie.

'It's a cipher, a secret code, invented by Magnesia Hypoteca, the wife of one of the first commanders.'

Jake looked at the translated message: there were twenty-eight digits, nearly all numerals, divided into four groups of eight – the order of which didn't make any sense to him – followed by a single phrase of English: *Follow the shadow's hand.*

'Well, the numbers are obvious,' Jupitus purred. 'The first set refer to Topaz's date of birth: the nineteenth of September 1356.'

'Correct.' Galliana nodded.

Jake remembered Topaz telling him that she had been born in a campaign tent during the Battle of Poitiers in the Hundred Years War. History Keepers could be born in all sorts of eras, depending where their parents were stationed – or travelling to – at the time.

'The middle section,' Jupitus continued, 'presumably refers to geographical coordinates.'

'Indeed,' replied Galliana. 'In this case, an island in the Tyrrhenian Sea called Vulcano. And the final set presumably indicate the historical date the message came from.'

'Sorry – I haven't got my glasses on,' Rose piped up. 'What *is* the historical date?'

Jake was also dying to know – he could not read it from his end of the room, either.

'The tenth of May,' Galliana said, then added in a sombre voice, 'AD 27.' Some of the agents glanced anxiously at each other as she continued, 'The date would make sense as we have recently picked up a quantity of Meslith chatter linking those coordinates with Agata Zeldt – a figure who has been silent for years.'

Now there were gasps around the table. Alan accidentally dropped his coffee cup into his saucer with a clatter.

Jake felt his stomach flip. He had heard all about the diabolical Agata on his mission to Venice. She was, in Charlie's words, *The most evil woman in history*; the monster who, as a child, had tried to drown her younger brother in a freezing lake; who had taught her maid a lesson by forcing her to sit naked on a throne of red-hot iron until she burned to death. She was also – and this was the most disturbing fact of all – Topaz's *real* mother. Of course, Topaz had disowned her completely – at the age of five she'd had the strength of mind to defect to Point Zero – but they were related by blood.

Rose put up her hand. 'Does anyone know what *follow the shadow's hand* means?'

It was clear from the blank faces that no one had a clue.

'And, more to the point,' said Jupitus, 'how do

we know it has actually come from Topaz? Perhaps Agata sent it herself—'

The double doors flew open. 'Sorry – I came as soon as I heard!' Nathan strode into the room. The sight of him brought an amazed smile to Jake's face: his clothes and hair were dripping wet, a rope and a harpoon hung from his shoulder and he carried a dead swordfish in one hand and a conger eel in the other, the latter trailing across the floor behind him. 'I hope I haven't missed too much; the conger was particularly tricky to land.'

'He has no shame,' Charlie muttered in horror, looking at the dead fish. 'No shame at all.'

'These may look grisly,' Nathan announced, chuckling at all the squeamish faces, 'but they'll make a change from roast chicken.'

Galliana groaned wearily. 'Thank you, Agent Wylder. Most thoughtful . . . Now, if you would put them down and take a seat . . .'

Nathan deposited his catch on a side table. 'By the way,' he said, ignoring the invitation and going over to the window, 'is there any reason why there's an elephant wandering around on the pier? For a while I thought I was imagining things, that it couldn't possibly be real, until it – how can I put this politely? – until it dispensed a particularly noxious parcel, which I can assure you was very real – *way* too real for early Tuesday morning.'

'It belongs to Oceane Noire,' Galliana snapped. 'If you had read the daily communiqué, you would know. Now sit down!'

Nathan looked shame-faced and took a seat next to Jupitus. 'So, news from Topaz, I hear.' He flashed his smile as he looked at the list of numbers, understanding their relevance immediately. 'Good gracious, she *is* a long way away. Are we sure it came from her?'

Galliana took a calming deep breath and addressed everyone. 'The fact of the matter is, though the use of the Hypoteca code would suggest that it is authentic, we have no *absolute* guarantee that this was written by Topaz. But that said, given that she would contact us only when she had *absolutely vital* information concerning the enemy – that was her original brief – I have decided to send a team to these coordinates to investigate. It goes without saying that travelling back one thousand, seven hundred and ninety-three years to AD 27 is an extremely gruelling undertaking so I can send only those of first-rate valour.' Galliana took a deep breath. 'I assign Nathan Wylder—'

'*Qui est le champion?!*' Nathan punched the air. His French accent was truly appalling.

'– and Charlie Chieverley.' Charlie just nodded soberly. 'Group leader—'

'I assume will be myself?' Nathan interrupted.

'– will be Jupitus Cole,' Galliana finished her sentence.

There was another round of murmurs. Jupitus coolly took a sip of coffee. Some of the older agents around the table – Dr Chatterju, and Signor Gondolfino, the head costumier, in particular – glanced at him with a hint of envy: once a keeper's valour had matured, he or she was rarely invited on the type of exciting mission they had taken part in when they were young.

Nathan put his hand up. 'Commander . . . is it not somewhat unusual to send an agent of Mr Cole's' – he chose the word carefully – '*experience* on a mission so far back in time?'

'If you're referring to his age,' Galliana replied, 'Mr Cole tested his valour only yesterday and his scores were off the chart – even better than yours.'

At this point Jupitus couldn't hide his sly smile. Try as she might, Rose was unable to conceal her admiration. Nathan was silenced: even he wouldn't dare put up a fight against the venerable keeper.

'You will sail tonight on the *Hippocampus*, a Roman merchant ship—'

'The *Hippocampus* . . .' Jake repeated the name to himself; it sounded intriguing, familiar.

'Tonight?' Nathan interrupted. 'Any reason we can't get going immediately?'

'A compelling reason, yes,' Galliana answered drily. 'The *Hippocampus* will not be delivered from the Calais workshop until late afternoon.'

'I get you,' Nathan said. 'They're souping it up – good to hear!'

Galliana looked down, indicating points on the map. 'You will take the Brest horizon point, vault to Sardinia East, and from there make your way to the Aeolian Islands. Your final destination is the islet of Vulcano. Is that clear?'

'Crystal,' Nathan replied.

Everyone else murmured their agreement – everyone except Jake, who stared solemnly at the floor. The first time he had attended a meeting, he had put up his hand and volunteered to join the mission to Venice. His offer had been flatly rejected, humiliatingly so. He knew that if he suggested joining *this* expedition, the rebuff – given the importance of the mission, the huge time span to be crossed, not to mention his failure in Stockholm – would be more resounding still. Despite this, his thirst for adventure, his need to be – at the very least – part of the mission to save Topaz was too strong. He tentatively raised his arm and spoke in the deepest voice he could muster. 'May I say something, Commander?'

There was an uncomfortable shifting amongst the History Keepers. Miriam looked at her son apprehensively. Charlie occupied himself by reaching for another brioche. Jupitus went so far as to roll his eyes heavenward.

'Commander, I am aware that I have brought dishonour to this service.' Jake turned to the rest of the room. 'I should tell you all now that it was I, and no one else, who was responsible for losing the atomium in Stockholm.'

There were more murmurs.

'I disobeyed orders and made a mistake for which I will never forgive myself – not until I have somehow, someday, put the situation right again.' He took a deep breath and saw that his mother was becoming increasingly anxious. 'I am aware also that this is a very hazardous and crucial assignment for which I am sure you consider me unworthy, but I beg you to offer me one last chance to prove myself. If you send me on this mission, I promise I will not let you down—'

'This is ridiculous!' interjected Jupitus, getting to his feet to make his point. 'Not just ridiculous – insulting! It shows a total lack of respect for the work that we do here.'

'Calm down, Jupitus – don't get your knickers in a twist,' Rose retorted, protective of her nephew.

'I am perfectly calm!' Jupitus hissed, then carried on, 'This secret service has operated for decades, for *centuries*, with strict tried-and-tested systems. No agent ever goes out in the field until he has had the most intense and thorough training. Then this *boy* appears and thinks he can do everything by his own rules. He already contravened orders by stowing away on the Venetian mission—'

'And as a result' – Alan was now ready to join the fray – 'did more to stop Zeldt than anyone else!'

'He then pushes his way onto the Stockholm operation' – Jupitus continued his diatribe – 'turns it into a farce, threatens our very existence, and now has the gall to stand here and volunteer again. If he was working for Zeldt himself, he couldn't make a better job of destroying us.'

Now nearly everyone in the room got caught up in the argument, all voicing their opinions loudly. Galliana did not interrupt, but listened judiciously.

Nathan leaned over towards her. 'Commander, would you allow me to say something? I may be able to resolve this.' Galliana nodded her consent.

'Listen . . .' He stood up. 'Listen to me, every-one.' When he wanted to be serious, Nathan – with a charm and authority beyond his years – was able to command respect. The keepers quietened down. 'Maybe Mr Cole is right, maybe Jake has disobeyed orders in the past, but I can tell you that he acted impeccably in Italy and Germany – even in Sweden. As I have already informed the commander, he warned us of an impending threat, and tragically I paid no heed. I envy his natural flair for what we do.'

'Hear, hear,' Charlie added.

'And maybe this *is* the wrong mission for Jake – in truth, I do think it is too far back for him – but it is still *incredibly* brave of him to volunteer.'

'Hear, hear.' Alan and Rose now joined Charlie in their agreement.

'And let's not forget, Mr Cole . . .' said Nathan, drawing to his conclusion. 'You yourself brought Jake into this dangerous world of ours, and I believe you owe him a little more guidance.'

It was clear from the silence that now descended that everyone agreed with Nathan. Even Jupitus looked remorseful. He sat down and sighed deeply.

Jake looked over at Nathan with a warm smile. Nathan winked back.

Galliana took charge again. 'Jake, Nathan Wylder is right: you have shown great courage. However, I must also agree that this assignment is not right for you.' Jake reddened as she looked at him before turning to the others. 'Agents Cole, Wylder and Chieverley – Signor Gondolfino will take you up for your fittings in the costumiery.'

'There's the rub.' Nathan turned to his neighbour. 'Roman fashion – it's a minefield.'

'Usually this would go without saying,' Galliana concluded, 'but I must ask you to treat your atomium consignment with the utmost care. We have only enough stock for a handful of journeys. You set sail at seven tonight.' And she stood to indicate that the meeting was over.

Just as everyone was bustling out, Oceane Noire

swanned in, the vast panniers of her dress sticking out on either side, her hair in a towering beehive. '*Qu'est-ce que s'est passé?* What's happened? Have I missed anything?' she asked the tide of chattering people coming the other way.

Rose, upset by recent matters, couldn't resist a dig at her old adversary. 'Yes, Jupitus is off to a beautiful island in the Tyrrhenian Sea – without you!'

She smiled curtly and exited as Oceane's expression turned to vinegar.

Jake went back to his room and threw himself down on his bed. Felson nestled in close, propped his head on the boy's knee and licked his hand.

When Jake was allocated this room after his return from Cologne, he had been told it was the one his brother had used whenever he visited Point Zero. Jake had searched through the drawers and cupboards for any sign of Philip. Of course, after three years, all his things had been removed or sent back to London, but Jake did find one item: wedged under the drawer of the little desk below the window was a photograph of the whole family at Christmas time – Jake, Philip, their mum and dad all smiling happily in the Djones kitchen in Greenwich.

Jake had not shown the photograph to his parents for fear of reviving sad memories, and kept it under his mattress. Now he pulled it out and examined it once again.

Philip was taller and broader than his brother. He was only fourteen in the photo, but already looked handsome and confident, with an adventurer's spark in his eye. He had his arm protectively round Jake, while Jake looked proudly up at him.

There was a soft knock on the door. 'It's Mum,' Miriam announced quietly. 'Can I come in?'

Jake slipped the photograph under the blanket as the door creaked open and she came in.

'How are you feeling, darling?'

Jake smiled and nodded. His mum came and sat on the bed. 'You're not too upset about Jupitus Cole, are you?'

Jake shrugged. 'He's entitled to an opinion.'

'Well, he's got a lot of those,' agreed Miriam. 'Dad and I never paid too much attention.' She took a deep breath. 'Listen, darling, I have some more bad news – we're going to have to go back to London.'

'What?' Jake felt his stomach flip again.

'We can stay a couple more days, then we need to pack up – the three of us and Rose too. Captain Macintyre has agreed to take us on the *Escape*.'

'Wh-why?' Jake stammered.

'Why? Because you need to get back to school, to your friends. We need to get back to work. People are waiting for their bathrooms. Dolores Devises' overflow pipes were supposed to be fitted three weeks ago.'

Jake's face was thunderous. 'When I first met Jupitus Cole, he said that school was pointless, that *the world was the place to learn*.'

'Well, you see, just another of his opinions—'

'And your bathroom shop's a disaster. Only your friends order things there – out of pity – and most of them have to get it all fixed again after you've installed it.' Jake bit his tongue, immediately feeling awful, but unable to take back the words.

Miriam sighed. She reached out and took his hand. 'I know all this seems very exciting to you. And it *is* exciting, it's a roller coaster, but it's also dangerous – so very, very dangerous. I couldn't bear it if anything happened to you.'

'All because of what happened in Stockholm?'

'No! We decided this before you even went there. We wanted to tell you last night, but it didn't seem the right time. Jake, you can't stay here. None of us can.'

He looked steadfastly down at his hands, his face crimson. 'It's not fair – you had *your* chance, you travelled all round history, you went everywhere . . .'

Miriam saw something sticking out from under the blanket. She picked up the photograph. The moment she set eyes on it, her face froze with both joy and unbearable pain. She stared down at her elder son, who was arm in arm with Jake, smiling so happily. It was a while before she said anything.

'Look at the state of that Christmas tree,' she murmured finally, deliberately making light of the situation. 'Your dad's tinsel obsession is verging on the criminal.'

At length she gave the photo back to Jake and wiped the tears from her eyes. She kissed him on the cheek and stood up. 'I'm sorry, darling, we have to leave by Friday,' she said, then left the room and closed the door behind her.

5 THE *HIPPOCAMPUS*

As the sun was setting over the mount, a bell rang to announce the departure of the agents. Jake was in the stables, where he had spent most of the afternoon with Oceane's elephant – now christened Dora – and the other circus animals. In return for apple treats, Dora had shown Jake some of her tricks – in particular, balancing a ball on her trunk and standing on her hind legs. They had developed an immediate rapport.

Before that, Jake had spent most of the day alone, shunning company. He felt desperately sad, as if he didn't belong there any more. Earlier that morning, after their fitting in the costumiery, Charlie and Nathan had come to find him, asking whether he wanted to join them for sword practice in the armoury. Jake had told them that he wasn't really up to it – he had to take Felson for a walk anyway.

As the bell tolled, he wondered if he even had the courage to go down and say goodbye to the others. 'You have no choice in the matter,' he finally told himself, and set off along the path that led to the quayside.

As he came down the steps, he saw that a small group of people had already gathered there. Some were carrying lanterns and there was an atmosphere of excitement. The ship they were looking at was very simple – quite different from the rest of the keepers' fleet. Her hull was fashioned from light, sun-bleached timbers; her prow was steep, like that of a Viking longship, and she had two square sails in cream and blue stripes. One was very large and attached to the mainmast (along with the triangular topsail); the other was much smaller and hung over the prow. A neat, square timber structure stood at the stern.

As Jake stared at her, a peculiar feeling came over him: his mind was filled with curious images – brilliant sunlight shining down on a palm-fringed bay, stacks of old amphorae, a cloud of sweet incense wafting on the warm wind. 'Incense?' he said to himself. 'When have I ever smelled incense?'

The ship seemed familiar, as if he had seen it some-where in a dream.

'There he is,' Rose exclaimed, holding out her arms to him. 'We were about to come and find you.' She was standing with Miriam, Alan, Galliana and Signor Gondolfino – who was wrapped in an elegant cape against the chilly evening air. Oceane Noire stood haughtily apart from the rest, her lion cub at her side in its new diamond collar.

'All right, darling?' Miriam asked Jake hopefully.

He nodded and continued to study the ship. Her name was inscribed in faded letters on the stern. '*Hippocampus*?' he said softly to himself. She still seemed familiar to him. 'What *is* a hippocampus?' he asked his dad.

'Interesting fact.' Alan clapped his hands. '*Hippocampus* is Latin for seahorse, but *also* the name of the part of the brain to do with memory.'

Jake started to work his way along to the prow; as he did so, vivid images came into his head – scales carved in wood and shining rubies. No sooner had this vision formed than he saw the figurehead curving up from the front of the ship – a creature with a long scaly neck and glinting red eyes. It was uncanny: he had imagined it precisely.

'Why do I recognize this ship?' he asked his parents.

Out of sight, behind his back, Miriam clutched her husband's hand. 'What's that, darling?' she trilled.

'This ship wasn't here when I came to Point Zero the first time – Galliana said it was in the workshop in Calais – so why does it seem familiar?'

Three faces – Rose's, Alan's and Miriam's – had frozen in perplexed smiles. 'I know!' Miriam said finally. 'The maritime museum in Greenwich – remember we went last year? They've got a model of one just like this.'

'That's right,' Alan agreed, nodding enthusiastically.

Jake could usually tell when his parents were lying. This, he felt instinctively, was one of those occasions. However, there was no time to pursue the matter as the three departing agents were now coming down the steps.

'Oh, good gracious me,' gasped Rose. 'Just look at those legs!'

She was referring to Jupitus, who led the group. He was wearing a tunic, belted at the waist, that came down to his knobbly knees, revealing long,

82

ghostly pale limbs. On his feet were sandals and slung across his back was a leather holdall. Rose couldn't stop giggling: Jupitus looked so stiff and awkward in his informal garb.

For very different reasons, Oceane was also struggling to come to terms with the vision. She smiled as bravely as she could, and even clapped a little, but she was clearly embarrassed. If she had her way, Jupitus would never take off his trademark tail-coat and breeches, even to go to bed.

Behind him, Charlie looked much more at ease in a similar outfit, Mr Drake bouncing happily on his shoulder. Nathan brought up the rear in a typically ostentatious get-up. Over his tunic he wore a golden breastplate and a skirt of thick leather strips. On his head was a helmet – also in gold – with a feathery red plume. The sight of Nathan in such an amazing costume made Jake feel very jealous. His comrades were going off on an adventure to the ancient Roman world, a thrilling place of gladiators and charioteers; of conquerors, emperors and armies; of Roman baths and theatres; a place that Jake could only dream of – while he was headed for London, which would doubtless be damp and drizzly, and school.

'In case you were worried,' drawled Nathan as he

spotted Jake, 'this is just my goodbye outfit. None of it really goes.' Jake hadn't been worried about his outfit at all, but Nathan carried on regardless. 'You see, the leather lappets are actually Thracian' – he indicated the skirt – 'and the breastplate is pre-Empire. But what the heck?'

'Exactly,' Jake found himself agreeing. 'It's a great ensemble.'

'So, I hear you're leaving us?' Nathan blurted out. 'Charlie and I are not happy about that at all.' He leaned closer and whispered, 'We tried to persuade your parents otherwise, but they seem to have made up their minds.'

'Well, you know,' Jake mumbled, 'I'm three weeks behind in history.'

'Very funny . . .' Nathan replied, then, as Charlie came to join them, 'I wanted to give you this . . .' He presented Jake with a sword in a scabbard. Jake's eyes lit up: it was the same gleaming weapon, its hilt shaped like a dragon, that Jake had asked to borrow on his first keeper's voyage to Venice, 1506. Then, Nathan had refused point blank. Now he was giving it to him to keep.

'Are you sure?' Jake gasped, taking it carefully and admiring the fine craftsmanship.

'But you can only have it if you promise to come back.'

Jake nodded enthusiastically and thought he might burst into tears again.

'And this is a little something from me and Mr Drake . . .' Charlie handed Jake a leather pouch. He opened it to find a collection of beards and moustaches. 'That's my spare set – thought it might as well go to a good home.'

Jake threw his arms around Charlie to thank him, making Mr Drake squawk and puff up his feathers. He then turned to Nathan, giving him a great bear hug. 'Find Topaz, won't you?' he whispered in his ear. 'And wherever you go, keep a lookout for Philip.'

'We'll do our best,' Nathan promised, resisting the urge to straighten his clothes.

With a serious look in her eye, Galliana handed Jupitus the box that contained the atomium and the Horizon Cup. 'Be safe, be careful,' she said, her hand still clutching the case. He nodded and she let him take it.

'All aboard!' Jupitus called out as he made his way towards the gangplank.

Oceane rushed after him dramatically, dragging

Josephine along with her. 'You'll write, won't you? Just a little Meslith from time to time?' Jupitus responded with a curt nod. 'And I'll start preparations for the wedding! I was thinking *un thème classique*, with lots of nymphs and satyrs and acres of silk tulle?' He nodded again. 'Good luck, *mon amour*!' Oceane leaned forward and pecked him on the cheek.

Jupitus looked coolly down at the lioness. 'Be careful with that thing, won't you?' Before jumping aboard the *Hippocampus*, he turned and searched the quay for Rose. His eyes lingered on her for a minute, making her freeze in shock – then he shouted again, 'All aboard!'

Charlie and Nathan headed up the gangplank, Nathan gave a short 'impromptu' speech, and they cast off. Jake felt miserable. He longed to charge across the cobbles and leap onto the ship, but he knew it was pointless. He clenched both fists until he had his emotions under control again.

Rose was secretly battling a similar impulse to jump aboard. Ever since Jupitus had announced his engagement to Oceane, she had put any romantic thoughts about him firmly to the back of her mind. The look that he had just given her brought them surging back. She furiously twisted the bangles around her wrist as the ship moved away. Before long, the blue and white sails were already far out to sea.

Jake watched the *Hippocampus* until it was just a hazy shape on the horizon. Then a mist came in and it was gone – along with his hopes and dreams. 'The *Hippocampus* . . .' he repeated to himself. 'I know I've seen that ship before.'

The bell in the clock tower struck two. With Felson at his side and a lantern in his hand, Jake tiptoed down the corridor to the communications room. He checked that no one was watching, then slipped inside. The desks where the decoders usually sat were empty; the main Meslith machine – the *Meslith nucleus*, as it was known – stood in its glass case in the centre of the room, two inked quills poised over blank rolls of parchment in anticipation of the next message from history.

'This way,' he whispered to the dog as he headed for another door on the far side, carefully opened it and went in. He shone his lantern around the long vaulted room, lined from floor to ceiling with shelf after shelf of ancient leather-bound tomes. It was reminiscent of the London bureau below the Monument, with its succession of study tables adorned with globes, but these ones were lit by the pale moonlight shining through the skylights.

After his mission to Venice and Germany, and before the Stockholm debacle, Jake had spent two weeks at Point Zero, getting to know the island and all its secrets a little better. He had been shown the testing chamber – a room with tapestry-covered walls and a mass of scientific equipment, where an agent's valour could be analysed and assessed – and the assault vault, a labyrinth of spiral staircases and stone passageways where training exercises were carried out. This vault, accessed through the armoury, had reminded Jake of a ghost train at a fair, with its flying arrows, slicing swords and life-size 'enemy' puppets jumping out or shooting up from the floor.

Jake had also discovered the archives, where records were kept – not only log books of every mission and journey undertaken, but also precise accounts of the weather throughout time, as well as tide tables, moon tables, sunrises, population statistics and a host of other information. Here you could find out, for example, how many people lived in Cadiz in 1740, how warm their summer was and what they were eating for lunch.

This was the room into which Jake and Felson, having waited for everyone to retire, had now crept. If Jake was to be denied an assignment, he had decided he would set himself one: he wanted to find out more about the *Hippocampus* – why it seemed so familiar and why his parents were so evasive about it.

At the far end was the section that detailed all the sea voyages – which ships had been used and to which destinations. The volumes – the spines imprinted with the History Keepers' symbol of planets whizzing around an hourglass – were arranged alphabetically: a series of twelve belonged to the *Barco Dorado*, another fifteen to the *Campana*, twenty or so to the *Conqueror*, and so on. Jake noticed one book standing slightly proud of the others: it was the last in the series dedicated to the *Escape*, the ship on which he had first sailed from London – that fateful journey during which he had learned that he could travel through time. He took it down and flicked through its pages, each one densely inscribed with beautifully curling letters. The last entry brought a smile to his face:

at the end of the list of passenger names – *Jupitus Cole, Charlie Chieverley, Topaz St Honoré*, etc., etc., was his own: *Jake Djones, 14. So I'm leaving Point Zero,* Jake thought to himself, *but here's the proof, in black and white, that I'm a History Keeper.*

He put it back and found the records of the *Hippocampus* – only six volumes. Jake took down the first and started scanning its contents. There was nothing but a succession of unfamiliar names. The second had no more to offer. In the third, Galliana Goethe's name appeared a number of times. In the fourth he saw Jupitus Cole's, and then, to Jake's amazement, the name Djones started making an appearance. Alan, Miriam and Rose were all there, either travelling alone or together, on trips to Macedonia, Persia, Numidia, Ostia – even a trip to Londinium, as London was called during Roman times. Next to each entry was the agent's age at the time. It was odd for Jake to imagine his parents when they were only seventeen and eighteen. How different they must have been.

The fifth volume revealed further unfamiliar names, but on the second page of the sixth, Jake got a shock: listed amongst the passengers on a mission to Cagliari in Sardinia in AD 121 was *Philip Djones,*

14. Jake ran his finger over the inscription as if it could somehow connect him with his lost brother. He carefully scanned the remaining records, but that was the only mention of him.

Jake was just returning the tome to the shelf when Felson started growling quietly, eyes fixed on the far end of the room. 'What is it?' Jake asked. The dog's growl deepened and he started to curl his lip and bare his teeth. A table scraped on the floor in the communications room. Just as Jake started looking around for a place to hide, the door began to creak open. At first it seemed as if the visitor was a ghost. Then Jake realized that it was an animal – he glimpsed dark golden fur. The creature padded into view – a lioness cub with a menacing look in her eye. Josephine stopped dead when she caught sight of Jake and his companion. There was a moment of frozen silence; then she gave a low snarl and began to advance towards them. Felson also pressed forward, protective of his master, eyes narrowed, teeth bared.

'Stay there – that's a good boy,' Jake commanded quietly, quickly scanning the room for another exit; there was nothing but book shelves on all sides. Then everything happened at once: Josephine shot forward, Felson intercepted her, the lioness's giant paws came down on him; and they tumbled to the floor in a tangle of limbs, both snarling savagely.

'Felson!' Jake shouted in terror, rushing to intercept them as the dog gave a yelp.

Then another voice boomed out: 'Josephine, *arrête*!' Oceane Noire swept into the room. '*Arrête tout de suite!*' she shouted. She was carrying an old book, which she hurled at the lioness, who reluctantly let go of Felson. Oceane was holding a lantern in front of her face and didn't notice Jake at first. 'What's going on?' she demanded of her pet. 'Why is this stupid dog here?' It wasn't until she had pulled Josephine away by her diamond collar that she became aware of another figure, half hidden behind a globe. 'You?' she said, stiffening.

'You should keep your animal under control,' Jake replied firmly, putting his arm around Felson, who was trembling with fear.

'That mutt of yours must have frightened her. She's sensitive, you know – just a little baby.' Oceane ran her hand along the creature's back. 'What are you doing here anyway?'

'I could ask you the same question,' Jake replied, kneeling down to pick up the book that she had thrown. It was a small, thick, leather-bound tome with an engraving of a palm tree on the front.

'Give that to me,' Oceane snapped, stepping forward and snatching it back. She stuffed it into her bag, then smiled sourly. 'As far as I know, the archives are for everyone,' she said sarcastically. 'When I can't sleep, I find it very calming to come here and peruse ancient records.'

Jake found this hard to believe but did not comment. 'Well, we'll leave you to it.' He edged round her, Felson glued to his side, and headed back towards the door.

'I hear you and your *family*' – Oceane managed to make the word sound insulting – 'are to return to London . . . Good luck with that,' she hissed.

'*Bonne nuit, mademoiselle.*' Jake nodded politely and left.

'*Good luck with that?*' he repeated to himself as he crossed the communications room. The whole encounter had been unnerving, but Oceane's parting comment had sent a chill down his spine. 'She's up to something – I can feel it.'

6 CATASTROPHE SICILIANO

From the moment Jupitus, Nathan and Charlie entered the horizon point in the calm seas of the 1820s, they had realized they had a problem. When the Constantor rings were aligned, they had all felt as if a bomb had detonated inside them; as if their bodies – their skin and bones – had been torn asunder and sent flying in every direction. Usually the feeling was dramatic but exhilarating; on this occasion it had been sickening and violent. One second they had been drifting in a vacuum of pitch-blackness, the next spiralling towards the ocean like a crashing jet, or shooting towards each other at breakneck speed.

By the time it was over and they had returned to consciousness on the deck of the *Hippocampus*, they realized that their problems had only just begun.

Now all three looked around in terror. They had arrived in the seas of AD 27 . . . in the middle of a cyclone.

The Mediterranean was a seething mass of black hills and roiling foam; the sky was dark and heavy as lead. It seemed for all the world like night, but Charlie spied, far in the distance, a tiny patch of hazy light where the sun was descending towards the horizon.

'Watch out!' Jupitus cried out over the maelstrom, his eyes widening in terror. Charlie and Nathan turned to see a vast chasm open up beneath them. The great mast tilted, creaking, and the whole ship plunged down into the trough. The agents clung to the rail as a colossal wave broke over their heads and spewed down upon the deck, drenching them instantly.

'Which course?' Nathan shouted over the tempest. He was at the helm, legs apart to steady him. Of the three of them, he looked most at ease, but there was fear in his eyes.

Jupitus tried to balance long enough to unfurl the map he clenched in his hand. Suddenly the ship lurched again, the mast swinging from side to side like a giant metronome. Jupitus lost his footing and tumbled across the deck. As he picked himself up, there was another sickening lurch, accompanied by a screech of howling wind. The map was ripped out of his hand and swept upwards. Nathan's reactions were lightning quick: he vaulted up onto the wheel and plucked it out of the air.

Jupitus, his eyes bloodshot, his face pale green, clawed his way to the helm. He was suffering not only from nausea, but also from guilt. As group leader, it had been his duty to check the weather records before they set off. These were not always a hundred per cent accurate, especially as far back as AD 27, but they would certainly have mentioned a storm of this magnitude. But the truth was, he had been so preoccupied with the prospect of embarking on such a mission, so far back in history, after all these years, that he had completely forgotten to do the checks. He was painfully aware that Nathan and Charlie would know exactly who was at fault.

'May I suggest, sir,' Nathan shouted over the wind, 'lowering the mainsail? The engine will do us more good than the wind.' Jupitus nodded. 'Charlie . . .' Nathan gestured to demonstrate his point. Charlie set about unfastening sodden ropes and lowering the billowing sail. Mr Drake, who had gone below deck the moment they hit the stormy seas, watched him from under a hatch, looking miserable.

Nathan spread the map out across the wheel. Although it was soaking wet, it had a thin waxy coating and the shapes of landmasses were just discernible. 'We're here . . .' He pointed to a star in the middle of the sea, the symbol of the horizon point they had just travelled through. 'Vulcano is here' – he indicated a small island, first on the map, then with a vague gesture out to sea – 'in that direction. Unfortunately that's also where the worst of the storm seems to be.' He was right: the towering black clouds were streaked with pulses of lightning. 'I suggest we head south and make for Messina on the north coast of Sicily. There's a lighthouse that can guide us.'

'Yes,' Jupitus agreed grimly, 'make for Messina.'

'Changing coordinates to south, south-east,' Nathan bawled out to Charlie as he turned the wheel. The ship veered round with it.

Jupitus hung his head and murmured, 'I'm sorry, it's my fault.'

Nathan heard him clearly enough, even through the wind and rain, but he decided to have a bit of fun. 'What's that? What did you say?'

'I said I'm sorry,' the other repeated, cast down with the shame of it.

Nathan smiled and kept his eyes ahead. Just then the *Hippocampus* crested another huge wave and plunged down into an abyss. Jupitus held on for dear life, but by the time the ship had righted herself, he looked like a dead man. He could control his sickness no longer, his stomach mutinied, and the remains of fettuccini Alfredo – prepared an hour ago by Charlie to get them *into the Italian spirit* – surged back out of his mouth. Nathan ducked and watched aghast as it was swirled away by the wind.

The *Hippocampus* and her crew forged on, pursued by the storm. The sun sank below the horizon, and the darkness seemed to amplify the deafening roar. After fifty gruelling, nail-biting minutes (at one point the ship took on a mass of water that threatened to sink her altogether) they finally spotted a pulse of light in the distance.

'There – the lighthouse,' said Jupitus weakly, lifting his head from the rail. He was still chucking up – though now only bile and mucus. 'I think the worst is over,' he murmured, speaking of both the tempest and his own state of health.

But he was wrong: the worst hadn't even *begun*.

They were halfway towards the port of Messina, whose twinkling lights were now just visible, along with intermittent flashes from the lighthouse, when the wind suddenly dropped and the waves abated. Jupitus looked up hopefully, certain that his prophecy had come true. He was able to stand without support for the first time.

Charlie, at the stern, noticed everything going quiet; not a *still* quietness, but a taut, dense one that filled his ears. Mr Drake seemed to be experiencing the same sensation as he kept shaking his head to restore his hearing. Then Charlie saw an unusual shape rising up from the sea far behind them. He took out his telescope and examined it, squinting into the gloom.

'Hell's bells and Bathsheba!' he cried. He had seen something similar two years previously, on a trip to old New Orleans with Nathan and Truman Wylder (most memorable for the number of earplugs he had got through, with both Americans booming at each other all day long). This was the same twisting tube, the same rotating column of water and debris. 'Cyclone!' he shouted to the others, but the word stuck in his throat. 'Cyclone!' he tried again. 'Approaching due north.'

Nathan and Jupitus turned in unison to behold the spectre. It was gaining on them; its tight spout of water, like a giant luminous rope, advanced, retreated and advanced again.

'It's coming straight for us,' Nathan gasped. He looked ahead again, applied full throttle and forged on.

The waves started to build up once more, rolling and breaking in all directions. The calm was replaced first by an eerie whistling, then a low hum, followed by a sound like galloping hooves, and finally an unearthly rumble as the monster suddenly accelerated towards them. Charlie and Jupitus held their hands over their ears, unable to bear the pressure. They looked up in terror and saw a colossal vortex of water shooting up from the raging sea and spinning at three hundred miles an hour.

'Hold on, everyone!' Nathan called, clinging to the helm, his hair now almost standing on end. As Charlie clutched the rail with all his might, Jupitus tottered across the deck and down the steps below.

'I wouldn't advise that, sir. If the ship sinks, you'll go down with her,' the American yelled.

'The atomium is below, and the Meslith machine! We're doomed without them,' Jupitus shouted back, tumbling down the stairs into the main cabin. He spotted the Meslith machine, took Nathan's cloak from the back of a chair, and wrapped the machine in it. He looked around for the box that contained the atomium – it was nowhere to be seen. The ship tilted at a crazy angle and Jupitus flew across the room, his knees smashing against the door frame. As he picked himself up, the *Hippocampus* lurched again. He tried to make his way back, falling through another doorway into the second cabin and hitting his head on the far wall.

As the ship started to right herself once more, he saw the open box lying on the floor, a tiny bottle of atomium and the silver Horizon Cup visible in its velvet interior. Still clutching the Meslith machine, he grabbed the little box and stumbled up the steps onto the deck.

At this same moment the eye of the cyclone slid tipsily across the sea, finally focusing its might on the stricken *Hippocampus*. The suction started: a tarpaulin lying on the deck was whisked up into the funnel; a wooden bucket followed. Then the whole structure started to judder as it was lifted out of the water. Jupitus threw his arms around the mast.

Suddenly there was an ungodly creaking, a splintering of wood, and the mast broke in two. The top half took off, lurching up into the raging sky, yanking the mainsail with it. As it flapped away, the mass of ropes suddenly became entangled around Jupitus's legs, pulling him upwards. He was flipped upside down as the top half of the mast fought to rise into the air, stretched in a tug-of-war between cyclone and sea.

Neither Nathan nor Charlie had ever seen such a sight: it was a battle of the elements, weather versus gravity, with Jupitus at the epicentre.

He screamed out loud – a long, defiant curse – as the box of atomium was plucked out of his hands and went spinning into the vortex. Then it was gone, eaten up by the storm. He clung onto the tangle of ropes, his cheeks juddering, his eyes bulging. Then, as suddenly as it had appeared, the cyclone was gone, and Jupitus was deposited on the deck. Charlie looked up in horror as the broken mast thundered down on top of him.

Nathan stared, ashen-faced. One of Jupitus's legs was bent right back and his eyes were closed. He didn't appear to be breathing.

*　　*　　*

Jake was forcing down an almond croissant when the shocking news came from AD 27. He was sitting in the corner of Galliana's living room, dressed in his school uniform. It was horrible to be wearing those itchy trousers again – he had got used to the luxurious feel of the breeches he'd been wearing at Point Zero. He was almost beginning to understand Nathan's passion for clothes.

They were due to set sail for London in thirty minutes' time, and Rose had hurriedly organized a 'sending-off breakfast' in the commander's quarters. It was a genteel affair, with everyone making polite conversation and handing round plates of pastries. Rose, Alan and Miriam – the three of them squeezed together on an ottoman – were now dressed in their modern clothes, Jake's father in his trademark corduroy trousers and his mother in an old woolly jumper. Sitting beside them a familiar item: their red suitcase, which Jake had discovered when he first arrived here. Truman and Betty Wylder, Nathan's parents, had also joined the party, along with Signor Gondolfino and a smattering of others. Oceane Noire had declined to attend, pleading a phantom migraine, but this gave everyone an opportunity to gossip about her and her

103

ridiculous lioness. Jake hadn't told anyone of his encounter with the pair two nights previously, and now that he was leaving the Mont St Michel, there didn't seem any point.

He glanced around the room. He had been here once before, for tea with Rose, shortly after returning from Cologne. He had been entranced by its glass cabinets crammed with objects from different corners of history – everything from old clocks to jade figures to dinosaur bones. On that occasion, at Rose's insistence, Galliana had taken a violin from a case – an ancient, gleaming Stradivarius – and played a suite by Bach. Although she was an exceptional violinist, the sound had filled Jake with sadness: Philip had also played the violin – it was just one of his many skills, learned, it seemed, without really trying.

Jake saw the violin lying on Galliana's dining table. He turned away and looked out of the window. Down below on the pier, the *Escape* was being prepared for the journey.

Miriam had told Jake that they would be getting home exactly two weeks after he had first left London, in late February, just after half term. The thought of school horrified him. He couldn't help remembering Jupitus Cole's opinion on the subject: *Perhaps you would like to stay at that dull, insipid school of yours?* he had sneered. *Day after day of tedious study. Dates and equations . . . For what? To pass some pointless exams? To be rewarded with a tiresome, bland employment followed by a slow, meaningless death.*

Jake had never forgotten those words, and now they haunted him more than ever. As he was wondering if he would dare tell any of his classmates of his adventures, the double doors flew open and a decoder rushed in, sought out Galliana, and breathlessly presented her with a scroll.

Galliana put on her spectacles and examined it.

'What is it?' Rose asked. Galliana passed her the message, and she read it out loud: 'Hippocampus *down; atomium lost . . .*' There were worried glances. 'Dear me, that doesn't sound good . . . *Send reinforcements, port of Messina, urgent!*' Her face fell again as she came to the last phrase. *'Jupitus critical . . .* Critical?'

Alan took the message and put on his glasses to look at it. Miriam peered over his shoulder. 'Messina?' she asked. 'What happened to Vulcano?' There were puzzled faces.

Jake had nearly choked on his croissant. *Send reinforcements* – he had heard the phrase clearly. He wanted to put up his hand and volunteer straight away, but thought it would be better to keep quiet for the moment. Instead he sat up straight and looked attentively from one person to the next.

'What would you like me to do, Commander?' the decoder asked. 'Shall I call all agents to the stateroom?'

Galliana's brow furrowed as she thought through all the options. 'The problem is the distance,' she mused. 'AD 27 would be a stretch for any of us, without a young diamond to carry us.'

Jake didn't say it out loud, but thought: *I'm a young diamond! Send me – I'll carry you.* But no one was even looking at him.

At length the commander turned back to the decoder. 'Ask Dr Chatterju to set up the testing chamber and assemble all eligible agents there in half an hour. We'll see whose valour reads the strongest.'

Valour, Jake now knew, referred to an agent's ability to travel through time, those with the strongest being able to voyage the furthest (as well as support – or *carry* – the weaker-valoured agents

106

with them). The general rule was that valour was stronger in the young, particularly when they were diamonds. (Each keeper could see a shape in the darkness when they closed their eyes. Jake, along with the rest of his family, saw diamonds, though many agents saw only squares or irregular shapes.)

Galliana turned to Miriam, Alan and Rose. 'I hate to do this, but I may have to ask you to postpone your journey.' Immediately Jake felt a surge of excitement at the possibilities that had opened up. 'I hesitate to send you on any dangerous mission,' Galliana continued, 'but I may ask you to consider a routine assignment to deliver atomium. Would you mind testing along with everyone else?'

Alan and Miriam looked at each other uncertainly and shrugged. 'Well, we can't leave them stranded, can we?' Miriam said without a great deal of conviction, casting a worried glance in Jake's direction.

'If I'm up to it,' Rose stated with much more enthusiasm, 'you can count me in!'

'Good,' said Galliana, taking off her glasses and making to leave. 'I shall see you all presently. I must go down to the communications room.'

Jake stood up in the hope that she might realize that *he* was their best bet. But she didn't even notice him. She left, along with the decoder, under a cloud of worry.

'*Che dramma!*' Signor Gondolfino shook his head as he struggled up with the aid of his cane. He bestowed a crinkling smile on Rose. 'Your delicious breakfast is ruined.'

'Mum? Dad?' Jake felt compelled to speak. 'Shouldn't I be testing? I'm the only young diamond here.'

Miriam's face darkened immediately. 'No, Jake, absolutely not!' she said firmly. 'Tell him, Alan.'

Alan agreed sheepishly. 'Your mother's right – not a good idea.'

Although there was clearly no chance of Jake being considered for the mission, his parents finally agreed to let him accompany them to the testing chamber to witness the procedure. He persuaded them by making them feel guilty about possibly leaving him alone again, as they had in London. Jake needn't have bothered: Miriam and Alan were quietly hoping that someone else would be picked over them.

When they arrived, several people were already waiting, dressed in the clothes of the period of history from which they came. Jake recognized one – a dandyish man in a wide-brimmed hat and lacy cuffs who looked like one of the Three Musketeers – as the man he had sat next to at his first ever meeting in the stateroom. All of them were at least a decade older than Jake. Some, such as Truman Wylder, who came *to try his ancient hand*, were four times his age. They all looked very serious, and a handful were stretching as if preparing for a race.

The chamber – Jake had only seen it once, and then in semi-darkness – was a high-ceilinged, square room decorated with large tapestry panels depicting moments in history: battles, voyages and processions. The centre was dominated by a large machine that looked a little like a giant Constantor: at its core was a solid, semi-spherical compartment with a red-cushioned seat – large enough to accommodate one person. In orbit around it were three metallic rings, each of a different thickness and circumference. Beside this were a number of levers and control panels, and a shelf full of bottles of coloured liquid and measuring devices. Here, Dr Chatterju, wearing a white laboratory coat over his kaftan, was carefully mixing a solution in a glass vial. His assistant – his young nephew Amrit – was checking the metal rings.

At length Galliana swept in, along with Olive, her greyhound. 'Pay attention, everyone. I have selected an extremely distant destination for the test, even more so than AD 27. It will be the same for everyone. Dr Chatterju, is the atomium replica blended and ready?'

Chatterju nodded. 'The participants will need to brace themselves.' He held up the vial and inspected it. Jake could see that it contained a quantity of luminous purple liquid that emitted violet steam. The scientist cast his twinkling eyes around the room. 'Who is to volunteer first?'

The dandyish musketeer stepped forward and doffed his wide-brimmed hat.

Galliana nodded. 'Thank you, Monsieur Belverre. When you're ready . . .'

Jake watched carefully as Belverre drank his dose of liquid. Amrit helped him up into the seat of the spherical compartment, carefully secured his arms and legs with velvet straps and placed a pair of large, dark, horn-rimmed glasses in front of his eyes.

'Enjoy the journey.' Dr Chatterju smiled as he

pulled a golden lever next to the machine.

The three rings started to rotate, each at a different angle, slowly at first, but quickly picking up speed. Within seconds they were travelling so fast they were merely a blurry haze around the central core. Within this, Jake could see Belverre, his hands twitching and his head gently nodding as if he were dreaming.

'What's happening now?' Jake whispered to Rose, who was standing next to him.

'Well, it's all very technical, darling,' she told him, 'but somehow it tests our valour; our ability to travel to history.'

Dr Chatterju was on hand to clarify more scientifically. 'The purple liquid is replica atomium,' he explained (Jake loved the way he made every word sound interesting). 'An exact quantity has been mixed to take the subject to a precise destination – in this case, far, *far* back into deep time. The machine simulates the effects of a horizon point. The subject then simply observes the scene and describes his experience afterwards. It is from the clarity of this description that *valour* is then graded.'

'The clarity?' Jake repeated, not fully understanding.

'Some people see it as clear as crystal; some don't see anything at all.'

'And some people disappear altogether.' Rose hooted with laughter. 'Do you remember when Oceane Noire's aunt was given *real* atomium by mistake and ended up in the year 606, when the Mont St Michel was occupied by marauding Franks?'

'I was doing Amrit's job then,' Chatterju commented with a mischievous twinkle, 'so I wasn't entirely to blame. But I will *never* forget her face when we finally managed to track her down.'

After a few moments the rings slowed and then stopped. Amrit unstrapped Belverre and helped him down. The musketeer looked as if he was half drunk – bleary-eyed and unsteady on his feet. Chatterju took him to one side and sat him down, then started asking him a series of questions, while carefully noting down his answers.

Amrit was just about to help Miriam Djones into the seat when the door flew open and Oceane Noire stormed in. She nearly knocked Jake for six with her wide skirts as she swept over to Galliana, '*Je viens de recevoir des nouvelles tragiques* – I've just heard the tragic news.' She sighed dramatically, clutching her neck. 'My poor, poor Jupitus – I must go to him *tout de suite*!' She didn't wait for permission; simply pushed past Miriam and jumped up into the seat. She had to squeeze her huge panniers flat against her hips to fit in.

Galliana shook her head, unimpressed, but nodded at Amrit to continue.

As the rings on the machine started turning once again, Rose whispered mischievously to Jake, 'With any luck, she'll disappear like her aunt.'

After Oceane and Miriam had been tested (needless to say, Miriam got the giggles the moment she was strapped in and had to do some deep breathing exercises to calm down), the others took their turn. After each interview, Chatterju passed the scores to Galliana, who looked at them with increasing concern.

It was past midday by the time they had finished. Galliana talked to Chatterju in a low voice, then solemnly announced, 'I am sorry to say that only one person has succeeded in the test. Miriam, you were very close, but not quite strong enough for this distance – which leaves only Rose. As she is also trained in ship navigation for that era, I will certainly be sending her to the Tyrrhenian Sea.'

'*C'est ridicule!*' cried Oceane. 'There must be some mistake – my vision was as clear as crystal.'

Galliana was tired and worried – otherwise she might not have answered so curtly. 'Mademoiselle, your score was quite the worst of the lot.'

'Out of interest, how did I do?' Alan asked with a nervous smile.

Reluctantly the commander answered, 'Perhaps you were worn down by your time in the sixteenth century – but your reading was low.'

His smile froze. Jake hadn't often seen his father look humiliated and it hurt more deeply than if the shame had fallen on himself. Miriam squeezed her husband's hands.

Galliana carried on, 'As you all know, we never allow agents to travel alone, however routine the journey, so we will need to spread our net wider. I will contact a number of overseas agents. Hopefully we can find someone in the next twenty-four hours.'

Jake could hold back no longer. 'Commander, could I say something?' He didn't wait for an answer, but pushed through the crowd, deliberately avoiding eye contact with his parents. 'Given that the mission is – in your own words – a routine delivery, and that our agents are obviously in urgent need of atomium, would you at least consider testing me for the assignment? It would save a lot of time.'

Alan Djones sometimes said things without really thinking, as if his voice were independent of his mind. This was one of those occasions. 'Go on, Commander – give him another chance,' he blurted out.

'Alan!' Miriam clapped him on the shoulder. 'We discussed this, remember?'

'Mum, please just let me try.' Jake turned to her, beseeching. 'I understand that you're frightened and I know I have a lot to learn – *everything* to learn – to be a real History Keeper. But I've never been particularly good at anything else—'

'Not good at anything else?' she interrupted. 'What about science and art and basketball? And your geography thesis was the best in the class.'

'And even you couldn't read it, it was so boring. Mum, working for the History Keepers, being part of this amazing organization – it's something I think I can do . . . I want to do it . . .' He made his voice deeper and squared his shoulders. 'I *will* do it, one way or another.'

There was silence, then Miriam heaved a deep sigh. 'I'm just your mother – what do I matter?'

Jake knew this was the closest he was going to get to her consent. He kissed her on the cheek and turned hopefully to Galliana.

She scrutinized him, then nodded. 'No promises. We'll test you, that is all. Dr Chatterju, one last measure, please.'

'Thank you, Commander, thank you!' Jake exclaimed excitedly, stepping forward to take his dose.

As Chatterju passed him the small vial of steaming purple liquid, he whispered roguishly in Jake's ear, 'Actually I had a dose standing by – just in case.'

Jake smiled conspiratorially and drank it down quickly. He had braced himself, assuming that it would taste as repulsive as genuine atomium, but actually it had a sweet citrus flavour.

Without waiting for assistance from Amrit, he leaped up into the cushioned seat. His legs and arms were duly fastened and the glasses positioned in front of his eyes. These were mirrored on the inside, and Jake could dimly make out his own honey-brown pupils staring back at him. Then he heard the soft whirr of the three spinning rings as they began to accelerate. Suddenly he felt a cool breeze in his face. He was overcome with a drowsy numbness and his eyes grew heavier and heavier. Just as it seemed as if he would fall into a deep sleep, brightness suddenly filled his vision and he jolted upright. He found himself in an extraordinary place . . .

7 A New Beginning

He was moving under a canopy of palm trees towards brilliant sunlight. Soft sand muffled his footsteps. The air was no longer cool but scorchingly hot – or certainly it felt hot; Jake wasn't sure if it was just an illusion. He came to the edge of the palms, stopped and surveyed the scene.

Ahead of him lay a palace compound – a low, sprawling group of buildings connected by shady colonnades. It was surrounded by clusters of tall palm trees, and its vibrant red walls stood out against the intense turquoise sky. Beyond it and on either side there was desert – an endless succession of softly undulating dunes shimmering far into the distance.

Suddenly there was a squawking sound that made Jake start. A bird took off from the palms behind him and soared over his head and out over

118

the desert. It was a beautiful creature, glistening like a jewel in the sunlight, wings of emerald green stretched wide. As it glided into the distance, Jake saw a series of shapes on the horizon. They were hard to distinguish at first, as the air danced in the heat; but as he looked closer he made out three triangles, similarly proportioned, one smaller than the other two.

'The pyramids . . .?' Jake murmured in wonder. 'The pyramids of Egypt . . .' As he gazed at the ancient structures, serene and alone in the vast landscape, utterly untouched by the modern world, he felt a sudden surge of emotion. His heart swelled and a tear came to his eye. 'History is amazing . . .' he whispered solemnly. 'Just amazing!'

The sun was burning into him like a blowtorch. His throat was parched and he needed water, so he started to make his way across the sand towards the palace – a fourteen-year-old boy in his school uniform, with just his shadow for company in this vast landscape.

He approached the striking entrance – triple-height wooden doors riveted with silver straps. These were flanked on either side by a towering statue: two giant golden figures with human bodies and animal heads. Each held its forearm imperiously across its chest, clutching a sceptre in its hand. Jake squinted up at their heads, with their long snouts and pointed ears; he was completely dwarfed by them – his head only came up to their knees.

He pushed open the doors, stepped into the echoey coolness of the interior and followed a wide marble passageway into a large atrium. He had visited ancient buildings before (just last year, on a dismally wet Tuesday, his class had gone to look at some dusty Roman mosaics), but he always found it hard to imagine what they would have *actually* looked like when they were first built: ruins, by definition, are worn and drab. The first thing that Jake noticed here was that it was full of colour.

On all sides were rows of stone columns, painted every colour of the rainbow: carmine, indigo, cerulean blue, dark lavender, lapis green and cadmium red. Beyond the columns, the walls were covered in intricate hieroglyphics, a million vivid symbols: birds, beetles, moons and countless other images. Cats dozed in the shadows. One got up, arched its back, stretched its legs, then curled up to sleep some more.

In the centre of the room, open to the sky, there

was a square pond, around which incense burners gave off a scent of jasmine. Jake went to examine it, kneeling down and sinking his hands into the water. His throat was now as dry as paper and he wanted to scoop some up to drink; but the water, like everything else, was just a vivid illusion.

The only piece of furniture was a spindly-legged table bearing a number of parchment scrolls. Jake went over to examine one that had been unfurled and weighed down at the corners with stones. It was a map – certainly the oldest he had ever seen – showing the twisting Nile and the little towns that lay along it. He was just bending down to study it more closely when he heard the sound of quick footsteps coming along one of the passageways.

Jake turned round as a number of guards filed into the chamber. They were dark-skinned, lithe and strong, and carried swords with distinctive curved blades; they wore leather breastplates, thick sandals and bronze helmets. Jake edged back behind a pillar as they started to check around, but it seemed that he was invisible to them. In fact, one walked straight through him. Their search complete, the guards stood to attention as soft pattering footsteps approached: five young ladies appeared, in pleated white dresses, with belts and neckpieces as colourful and elaborate as the painted columns.

The last figure to enter clearly commanded respect – everyone bowed as she came in. She was shorter and slighter than the rest, but she seemed to fill the space with an aura of power. In her bare feet she stepped over to the table and looked at the map, then, without turning round, addressed her retinue. To Jake's ears her voice sounded as foreign and musical as birdsong.

He stepped forward to examine her more closely. He knew he was invisible – he knew he was actually sitting inside a piece of apparatus in a room in Normandy – but he was frightened of this tiny woman who radiated such authority. She wore a headdress fashioned in the shape of a bird, just like the emerald-winged one he had seen before entering the palace. Her skin was as pale as marble, her lips as red as strawberries, her eyes as dark and dazzling as jet.

As Jake gazed into them, he felt a cool rush of air. All at once he was aware of golden rings rotating around him, and the woman's eyes started to fade – until all that remained were two shining black pupils; then, with a pop, those also disappeared.

Jake found himself once more in the testing room, with his parents and all the other agents peering at him.

'All right, darling?' Miriam asked hesitantly. 'You were certainly shaking around a lot.'

Jake nodded blearily, stunned by the sudden transition from a bright palace in Egypt to this dimly lit chamber with its dark tapestries. Amrit untied the straps and helped Jake down. Then Dr Chatterju stepped forward with his notepad, smiling warmly. He looked down through his round spectacles and started asking all sorts of questions about the journey Jake had just taken.

Jake needed no coaxing; he described everything in detail, from the palm trees to the palace, the bird, the pyramids ('You actually *saw* them?' Alan exclaimed out loud. 'No one ever *sees* them!'), the courtyard, the pond, the map and the women. With each additional piece of information, the group around him grew more and more astonished, some shaking their heads in disbelief.

'*C'est impossible!*' Oceane snorted when Jake gave the exact colour and form of the imperious lady's headdress.

After a while Chatterju, who had been scribbling

furiously, trying to keep up with Jake, shook his head and put down his notepad. When the boy finished, the other agents were all looking at him in amazement.

'So?' he asked them. 'Did I pass?'

Galliana took a deep breath and looked at Miriam with a questioning eye. It was Alan, however, who spoke first. 'Did you pass?!' He stepped forward and threw an arm round his son. 'Did you ever! I've never heard the like! Not even Nathan Wylder can see so much detail in a test that far back.'

Jake rewarded himself with the glimmer of a smile as his dad pinched his cheek proudly. 'He's an adventurer, Miriam,' he said with a tear in his eye. 'Our boy's an adventurer – nothing we can do about it!'

Miriam just stared back at him, stony-faced.

Galliana nodded at Jake. 'Congratulations. You just travelled to 1350 BC. The test proves that you could travel there in real time – although, of course, the actual journey would not be so pleasant. You have an uncommon talent, Jake.'

At this point Oceane Noire had heard enough. 'I must go and feed Josephine, she'll be starving,' she announced, and flounced out of the room, bumping into Jake with her panniers again. No one paid her any attention.

'1350 BC?' Jake murmured. 'That's . . . over two thousand years ago.'

'Three thousand, one hundred and seventy to be precise. Apart from Rose, all anyone else could make out was vague shapes.'

'And who was the lady at the end?' Jake asked. 'Was she real?'

'She was real once. I had the dubious pleasure of meeting her. She was charming, but as dangerous as a pit of vipers.'

'Cleopatra?' Jake asked excitedly. In truth she was the only famous Egyptian he knew.

'Dear me, no, not that troublemaker.' Galliana shook her head. 'And way before her time. It was Nefertiti.'

Jake took a deep breath. He drew himself up as tall as possible and affected his deepest, most grown-up voice. 'So does this mean I can go on the assignment with Rose?'

Galliana looked round at Miriam. For a moment there was silence, then Jake's mum shrugged and resigned herself to fate. She knew that, try as she might, she could not prevent her son becoming a History Keeper. 'It was the same with Philip,' she said quietly. 'The power was simply too strong.'

In less than an hour Jake and Rose were being fitted for their Roman outfits in the costumiery – Jake by Signor Gondolfino himself. He'd already been given a white tunic and sandals similar to the ones Charlie had worn, and now the tailor was carefully adjusting his brilliant-white toga.

Gondolfino was chatting to him: 'I'm dressing you as a young nobleman, the handsome son of a senator or some such. I've said it before, I will say it again' – his old eyes twinkled – '*bel viso*, such a face for history.' He fastened the toga in place with a gold pin and smoothed it down. 'Now, you'll need a sword of some description.' He was about to step over to a table where an assortment of Roman arms were laid out when Jake stopped him.

'Can I wear this one?' he asked hopefully, holding up the weapon Nathan had given him.

Gondolfino adjusted his eyeglass and examined the silver hilt in the shape of a dragon. 'Well, it's not strictly speaking the right period' – he shook his head – 'but it has some of the characteristics of the

126

gladius hispanus . . . perhaps we could just about get away with it.'

Jake excitedly fixed it to his belt.

'*Molto galante* – very gallant!' Gondolfino nodded, motioning for Jake to admire himself in the mirror. He looked at his reflection: a proud young Roman stood staring back at him.

On the next level up, Rose was being fitted with a dress, a Roman *stola*, by one of the other costumiers – a tall, haughty man in a checked jacket and breeches. Her hair had already been piled high up onto her head and studded with jewels. Once the costumier had secured a band around her waist he stood back to admire his creation. The dress made the most of Rose's curvaceous figure.

'Somewhat on the voluptuous side, wouldn't you say?' she chuckled as she mischievously slipped a leg through the split at the front of the dress and adopted an alluring pose.

'I think it's pleated perfection,' the costumier swooned, clasping his neck dramatically.

When they were finished, Jake and Rose quickly went down to the armoury. Dr Chatterju had asked them to pass by on their way to the harbour; he and Amrit were waiting next to the shooting gallery.

127

The doctor called them over to look at something in his hand. 'I have this for you to take to Sicily. It's the prototype hoisting device designed by Agent Nathan Wylder. He's been nagging me about it for months, so I dare say you had better give it to him now that it is finally operational.'

'Hoisting device?' Jake asked. He was perplexed: the object looked like a belt. It had a large golden buckle, fashioned in the shape of a lion's head, its eyes marked with jewels, one green and one blue and each minutely engraved with the History Keepers' logo of planets around an hourglass.

Chatterju demonstrated how it worked. He moved Jake to one side, aimed the buckle – like a gun – towards a wooden beam in the ceiling and pressed the blue eye. There was a sudden whistling sound as a small dart flew out of the mouth of the golden lion, trailing a thin wire. The dart struck the beam.

'Amrit, if you would be so kind . . . ?' The boy stepped forward and Chatterju tied the belt around his waist and fastened it tight. He then pressed the green eye. To Jake and Rose's amazement, Amrit – grin still firmly in place – started to ascend towards the beam, ratcheted up by the ingenious device until his head bumped into the ceiling. Even then, he carried on smiling.

'It's a feat of deceptively simple engineering.' Chatterju chuckled proudly. 'It could take the weight of Henry the Eighth – even in his heavy period.'

Amrit was lowered down and the wire wound back. Then the device was reset and handed to Rose.

On their way out of the armoury, Jake spotted something out of the corner of his eye. He looked straight ahead, pretending he hadn't seen it; but, hidden in the shadows behind a rack of weapons, a figure was watching them. The silhouette, with its huge panniers, was unmistakable: Oceane Noire.

'As soon as you arrive, you'll let us know, won't you?' Miriam asked Jake the moment he appeared on the quay. It was a sunny afternoon and a handful of well-wishers had gathered, including Dora the elephant and Felson, his ears pinned back anxiously at Jake's leaving.

'Yes, Mum.'

'And when you reach the horizon point, hold onto Rose *tightly* – do you understand? It's one thing going back millennia in the testing chamber;

the reality is a lot more terrifying. The first time I travelled that distance, I practically went into a coma.'

'She's right.' Alan nodded. 'Had to give her mouth-to-mouth resuscitation.' He patted his wife on the back. 'There are *some* benefits to the job.'

'I got it,' said Jake, tossing his bag onto the deck of the small ship that was waiting for them. He read her name – the *Conqueror* – written in faded gold letters. He remembered that Topaz had pointed her out to him when he first arrived on the mount, describing her as a Byzantine dhow. She was similar in shape to the *Hippocampus*, but much smaller, the size of a large fishing boat. Her square brown mainsail was decorated – also in faded gold – with the motif of a trident.

'I made you both some food for the journey,' Miriam continued brightly, handing her son a holdall containing various covered dishes. 'They just need heating up. I think I may have surpassed myself,' she added with a proud twinkle, before a tear came to her eye. 'You look ever so handsome, darling. Doesn't he, Alan?'

Alan gave his son a hug. 'We're proud of you,' he whispered in his ear.

'Mum, Dad, before I go, I need to tell you something.' Jake was suddenly very serious; he looked from one to the other, then lowered his voice. 'Will you keep an eye on Oceane Noire? I don't trust her. Someone passed on information about the Stockholm mission. Maybe *she's* the double agent?'

At this moment he and his parents spied her on the battlements above them. They watched as she leaned over the parapet, her back to them, and flicked open her fan.

'A double agent?' Miriam chuckled. 'That would actually mean doing some work.'

Jake leaned in closer. 'A couple of nights ago,' he whispered, 'I found her going into the archives in the middle of the night.'

'The archives?' Miriam frowned. 'What were *you* doing there in the middle of the night?'

Jake shrugged. 'It's a long story. We should talk about it another time. But Oceane was behaving really oddly. She was holding a book with a picture of a palm tree on it.'

'I don't think it's a crime to carry a book with a picture of a palm tree on it,' Miriam pointed out.

'She got into a terrible panic when I picked it up,' Jake persisted. 'As if she was hiding something.

131

And just now, in the armoury, she was watching us.' He put his hand on his mother's shoulder. 'Please, will you promise me – just look into it?'

'Of course we will, darling' – Miriam smiled – 'if you think it's important.'

Galliana gave a little speech, at the end of which she handed Rose the atomium for their journey. 'Guard it with your life,' she whispered to her old friend. 'Our situation is perilous.'

She watched as Rose carefully placed the consignment in her bulging carpetbag. Galliana knew that the luggage was completely wrong for ancient Rome, but said nothing, knowing that – like a talisman – Rose's carpetbag went everywhere with her, even to AD 27.

They all said their goodbyes. Jake was just heading up the gangplank when Felson padded forward hopefully. Jake knelt down and ran his hand across the great scarred head. 'I'll be back soon. Mum and Dad are going to look after you, along with Dora here.' The elephant showed willing by reaching out her trunk and playfully hooting in his ear.

Jake and Rose climbed aboard the *Conqueror* – as Rose was trained in navigation, they would sail her between the two of them – and cast off.

Rose felt a shiver of excitement. 'This is just the sort of boat I loved to take out back in the old days – sturdy and fast.'

Jake watched the party of people and animals on the shore as they became smaller and smaller. Even when Miriam had vanished to the size of a dot, he could see that she was still waving. Then she was gone, lost in the haze.

The wind filled the sails and buffeted Jake's hair. Once again he was overcome with the sheer thrill of the adventures that lay ahead. 'It feels amazing, doesn't it?' he shouted over to Rose, who was at the helm. 'Like a new beginning?'

Rose nodded, smiling determinedly, hiding from Jake her deep dread of the approaching horizon point. However many times she had done it in the past, however much she assured herself it would be all right, travelling into deep time filled her with terror.

On this occasion it turned out that her fears were justified.

8 OCEAN TO THE ANCIENT WORLD

The hour between taking the atomium and arriving at the horizon point was one of the most peculiar and sickening in Jake's life. As she handed him his dose with a shaking hand, Rose had warned him that no two journeys through the time flux were ever the same. 'There are so many variables,' she had said in ominous tones, 'and the further back in time, the more variables there are.' So, even though this was the sixth time Jake had taken the vile-tasting liquid, this episode was unique.

As usual, minutes afterwards, his head started to throb and he felt dizzy and disorientated; the sound of the sea became distant, and everything around him – the ship, the cabin, even Rose herself – seemed unreal. Uncomfortable as these sensations

134

were, he was familiar with them from previous journeys. Far more unsettling were the disturbing visions. Before, usually at the horizon point itself, Jake had glimpsed snapshots from history – the glimmer of a castle in the moonlight or a half-built cathedral. Those images were fleeting and strangely uplifting; the ones he experienced now were both diabolical and prolonged.

To begin with he heard a series of sounds: snorting horses, the clash of swords, bells tolling, distant cries – first of single people, then of multitudes. Then the noise grew, like bacteria, into *solid images*; suddenly Jake saw gory vignettes of war, of collapsing palaces, raging fires and thunderous earthquakes. He saw bloodthirsty horsemen storming a citadel; a group of wailing women escaping a massacre across a moonlit river; a procession of masked men being led to a scaffold in a snow-covered city; two vast armies charging towards each other across a valley. The sounds of battle were so loud that Jake had to cover his ears. And still the visions haunted him: skies cracking with thunder, fleets of ships sinking and graves filling with bodies.

After what seemed like a lifetime, the nightmares began to dissolve and Jake was once again aware of the ship, the wind and the sea. He felt normal enough to sit up – he was leaning against the balustrade at the prow – and check that Rose was all right. To his horror, he found that she was no longer on deck. The ship's helm was unmanned, the wheel turning this way and that. The rings of the Constantor were almost aligned, signifying that they were fast approaching the horizon point.

'Rose?!' he shouted out as he leaped to his feet. 'Rose, are you there?' He tore along to the stern and scanned the ocean. If the unthinkable had happened and she had somehow fallen overboard, he would need to know immediately – before he took off into the past. He couldn't see her, but he had no idea how long he had been in a trance. He looked again at the Constantor – the axes were closer still.

'Rose?' he yelled desperately as he jumped down the steps and into the main cabin; but it too was deserted. A lurch of panic was added to all Jake's other symptoms – his nausea, dizziness and thumping head. He threw open the door into the second cabin. There was no one in there either; the bunk beds were empty. Just as Jake felt himself dropping into a vortex of despair, he heard a moan and saw a sandaled foot sticking out from behind the bed.

'Rose, are you all right?' he said, rushing to her side.

At first she didn't notice Jake; she was in her own world, rocking deliriously from side to side, clutching her carpetbag.

'Rose, you have to get up. We're close to the horizon point.'

She became aware of a figure leaning over her and smiled. 'He loves me, you know . . . Jupitus Cole loves me.' Then her face darkened. 'But he's marrying Oceane Noire.'

'Rose, we don't have much time,' Jake insisted, trying to pull her to her feet.

'I thought I didn't love him,' she murmured, 'but now I'm not so sure . . .'

Jake thought she must be drunk and even looked around for an empty bottle. Then he remembered the time he had gone to Venice in 1506: he had started doing an Irish jig and ended up embracing Topaz on the prow of the *Campana. He* must have seemed drunk then.

Jake had another idea: he ran along to the galley and grabbed a glass of water, went back and – apologizing before he did so – tossed it in Rose's face. Charlie had done the same to him, and it had revived him immediately. Now the opposite was true: Rose's smile froze momentarily, then she passed out.

'Rose?' He shook her again, but she was unconscious. *All right, take the initiative*, Jake said to himself. *How hard can it be to enter a horizon point? I've seen them do it . . .*

He charged back up the steps, flew over to the helm and grabbed the wheel. It was heavy and seemed to have a will of its own; he had to use all his strength to turn it right, left and right again, until finally the golden rings were aligned.

The ship started to judder.

'Ten, nine, eight . . .' Jake counted down, holding onto the wheel with all his might. A whirlwind encircled him; colours flashed. He had only reached three when suddenly everything became silent, diamond shapes exploded outwards, and he took off like a missile into the sky.

Everything he had experienced in the last hour might have been horrific – the sickness, the appalling visions, the panic – but this moment was sheer magic; one of the most mysterious and breathtaking of Jake's life. He shot (or, at any rate, his alter ego did) noiselessly into the sky, as graceful and swift as an arrow, searing through the troposphere, the stratosphere and into the deep, deep blue of the thermosphere. The Earth shot away from him and, for the first time in his life, Jake saw the planet as a whole. As he gazed down at it – a shimmering blue ball in a never-ending firmament of twinkling stars – he felt calm. In that moment it struck him that on this little sphere below him, *all* of history had taken place – from modern-day London where he'd grown up, to the nineteenth-century Mont St Michel, to sixteenth-century Italy and Germany, to the Roman times to which he was now travelling. All this – and all the hundreds of civilizations beyond: the Greeks, the Phoenicians, the Assyrians, the ancient Chinese and Egyptians. That blue planet had been home to all those epochs and their glories – their art and learning, their progress and invention; their kings, conquerors, explorers and despots. It was a moment of profound wonder that Jake knew he would never forget.

Within seconds he was flying back to Earth. As he shot through the sky, the continents took shape once again: Africa and Europe formed beneath him. A moment later he was careering towards the Mediterranean. Finally he saw the *Conqueror*, all alone in a sparkling sea. He saw himself standing at the helm in his white toga, and Rose stumbling up the steps onto the deck. With a final rush, he returned to himself.

Jake looked around, squinting in the sunlight. The sky was completely different here – a brilliant cobalt blue – and the air was fresh and warm. Rose, still a little bleary-eyed, came and put her arms around her nephew.

'We made it!' she murmured. 'AD 27.' They looked at each other and she burst out laughing.

They set their course and sailed through the warm afternoon, serenely cutting across the sparkling sea. Rose felt groggy (travelling to history, she explained, was far more gruelling for adults than it was for youngsters), and Jake suggested that she lie down while he took the helm. She insisted that she was too excited to sleep but would give it a go. She settled down on some cushions, and within seconds she was snoring like a foghorn.

As the sun started to set and the sky turned from pink to maroon to indigo, Jake – while keeping an eye on the wheel – brought a table and two stools from the galley and set them up on deck. He laid the table with a white cloth, knives, forks, napkins, and a lantern that he found in a dusty cupboard. He heated up the dishes of food his mum had given him, lit the candles and finally woke Rose.

It took her a while to surface, but when she saw what Jake had done, she burst into tears. 'Sorry,' she sobbed, searching in her carpetbag for a tissue. 'A touch emotional this evening . . .'

Jake showed her to her seat like a professional waiter. 'Mum said she surpassed herself,' he said as he whipped off the dish covers. There was a moment of stunned silence as Jake and his aunt studied their contents, then they both burst out laughing. Each dish was burned to an unidentifiable cinder.

'All right, presentation may need some work,' Rose conceded, plunging a serving spoon through the outer crust of charcoal on one of them, 'but I'm sure it tastes delicious.' She served up two portions and they both ate with trepidation. Just one mouthful produced more uncertain giggles, followed by a discussion as to what the dish might or might not contain – 'Nuts? Bacon . . . ? Toenails?' – which brought fits of such uncontrollable guffaws that Rose had to leave the table, shaking her bangles, to take some calming air at the prow.

Feeling guilty about laughing at Miriam's expense, after dessert ('dread and butter pudding', Rose christened it) Jake and his aunt drank a heart-felt toast to her: 'To absent friends!' they exclaimed and clinked glasses.

As the stars began to light up all around, like some boundless celestial theatre, Rose closed her eyes and let the warm wind caress her face. She began to tell Jake about some of the missions she had undertaken in her youth – in particular an expedition to the mountains of Tibet in the ancient time of Kanishka, and another to Incan Peru, where she'd fallen in love with a handsome farmer in the emerald-green plains below Machu Picchu. 'Of course, it's hopeless falling for a civilian,' she sighed, misty eyed, 'because they can't go back with you. It's hard enough explaining you live on the other side of the world, let alone the other end of history.'

The word 'love' reminded Jake of what Rose had said earlier about Jupitus – *I thought I didn't love him, but now I'm not so sure.* He decided he didn't want to embarrass her by prying further, but he was desperate to know whether it was down to the effects of the atomium or was actually true. As he gazed up at the north star, pulsing gently in the heavens above him, he pondered his own feelings on the subject.

Up until a month ago, when Topaz St Honoré had come into his life, with her mysterious smile and her indigo eyes, love – *romantic* love, at any rate – was something he didn't understand at all. It had always seemed to require the unnecessary expenditure of such a lot of energy. He couldn't put it into words, but Jake felt differently now. Somehow the sheer existence of Topaz made him want to do things better; be braver and more daring. She didn't ask anything of him, but Jake felt nonetheless compelled to make the world a better and safer place. 'A better and safer place?' he said to himself, shaking his head. 'Where do I get these phrases from?'

At dawn the next morning Jake spied land on the horizon and called over to Rose, who was fast asleep under a blanket, her head cushioned by her carpetbag.

'Here already?' she cooed. 'I must have dozed off again.'

Jake couldn't help but smile: she had slept solidly through the night. The journey back in time really had knocked it out of her. She sat up, her corkscrew hair going off in every direction, and squinted into the distance.

Despite the sunrise the distant lighthouse still glimmered with fire, but he could see a big landmass ahead. The faint outline of a town was just discernible, beyond that rose a volcano in hues of shimmering purple. 'Mount Etna, looking majestic,' Rose sighed dreamily. She took a compact from her bag, opened it and examined her puffy eyes. 'Rose Djones, looking majestic too,' she added with a giggle.

As Jake steered the *Conqueror* on towards the harbour of Messina (he was increasingly enjoying navigating), he noticed another ship approaching from the other direction, her two dozen oars moving swiftly and perfectly in time. He gaped in awe as she sped past them, decks teeming with activity. There were several men – personal guards – many of them bearded, and each wearing a golden breastplate that glinted in the morning sun. At the stern, under an awning, an imperious-looking couple reclined on a large velvet divan. An attendant was fanning them with peacock feathers. The man, dressed in a brilliant white toga, had narrow eyes and dark walnut skin. His companion was thin-lipped and pale and clutched her neck as she gazed out across the seas.

'*Salvete, amici!*' Rose called out mischievously. One of the guards, a particularly burly and handsome man, smiled and winked back at her, but the haughty couple ignored her completely. 'If you thought Oceane Noire was bad,' she confided to Jake, 'Romans – some of them, anyway – take snobbery to a whole new level. But who can blame them? They're the first civilization in history to rule the world, practically from one end to the other.'

Once they had rounded the island on which the lighthouse stood (Jake noticed that its light was produced by *real* fire; dark smoke was rising up into the blue sky), the port started to take shape: a jumble of square white buildings with terracotta roofs, interspersed with clusters of cypresses and palms, spread up into the surrounding hills. The harbour itself was teeming with ships of all shapes and sizes, docking or setting sail, delivering or loading up amidst a cacophony of shouting people and squawking animals.

'If all has gone according to plan,' Rose said, coming over to Jake at the helm, 'the others should be waiting here. See if you can spot them while I try and bring this thing in safely – I need the practice. Parking has always been my downfall!'

As Rose took charge of the wheel, Jake stood at the prow and scanned the quayside for his friends. He was thrilled at the prospect of seeing them again. Jake had only known Nathan and Charlie for a matter of months, but he already felt that they were his best friends. When people of your own age are prepared to actually risk their lives for you – and you're prepared to do the same for them – it gives a different meaning to friendship.

Jake trembled with excitement as he surveyed the busy Messinians – an attractive people, robust and glowing from the Mediterranean sun – going about their morning business, all dressed in tunics, togas and sandals. He searched amongst them for Nathan's tall figure, for Charlie's crazy brown hair, even for Jupitus's thin and haughty silhouette. He gasped when he caught sight of a multicoloured parrot, but then realized he was sitting on the arm of an old fishmonger with a crinkled face, and was a totally different colour to Mr Drake, anyway.

As Rose drew closer, she crashed into nearly everything heading in the other direction. It took four increasingly embarrassing attempts for her to dock, each time mumbling profuse apologies to an assortment of angry Sicilians, until finally the ship bumped against the quayside. Now familiar with the routine, Jake jumped out and fastened the moorings.

'Any sign of them?' Rose asked.

Jake shook his head. 'Shall I go and have a proper look round?' he asked hopefully. As well as being keen to find the others, he was desperate to explore this new and exciting world.

'All right, but don't go too far.'

Jake headed along the dock, gazing in wonder at all the activity, taking in the myriad smells and sounds. Everywhere tradesmen and merchants were buying and selling – amphorae of wine, sacks of grain, vats of golden honey and crates of fresh olives. There were stalls selling pottery and glass, animal hides piled high, cloth and parchment. There were pyramids of powdered dye in brilliant colours – crimson, burnt umber, ultramarine and cadmium yellow. Traders sold marble, mosaic tesserae, ivory, gold and chunks of amber. Meat was being roasted over coals, and there were pens of *live* animals – sheep, goats and chickens.

Jake took it all in. Only one sight wiped the smile

off his face: a cage containing several terrified-looking humans. They were chained together, dressed in rags, their hair matted and their skin filthy. A pot-bellied man with black teeth and lank grey hair held a girl by the arm as he auctioned her off. She was even younger than Jake.

He was overcome – first with pity and then with anger. 'Slaves?' he murmured to himself, and stopped and stared, jaw clenched, at the pot-bellied man. When a prospective buyer – a man with a white beard – went to examine the girl's teeth, as if he were buying a horse, Jake found himself stepping forward in outrage.

It was at this moment that he saw the parrot staring at him. It was perched on a windowsill, and this time Jake was in no doubt about its plumage. 'Mr Drake?' he whispered.

The bird suddenly took off, flew over Jake's head and landed on the shoulder of someone in the crowd. At first Jake couldn't see who it was, but then his heart soared as Charlie appeared. Nathan was at his side, looking magnificent in his brilliant-white toga. They were both tanned from their week in the sun. Jake wanted to shout out to them at the top of his voice, but decided it would be wrong to attract attention, especially as he was still on trial as an agent for the History Keepers. So he waited patiently, assuming the most serious expression he could muster, his heart pounding beneath his tunic.

As it turned out, Jake needn't have worried about showing his emotions: the moment the three of them were face to face Nathan dropped his bag, stepped forward, took Jake in his arms and hugged him hard. Then Charlie did the same.

'How are you, Jake?' Nathan beamed. 'It's great to have you here.'

'Is it?' he asked with a tremulous smile.

'Of course it is – we missed you. You're looking very dashing in the tunic department.' Nathan reached out to get a feel of the fabric. 'I thought so . . . Egyptian cotton – light, durable and positively zinging on the eye. I can tell Gondolfino likes you. We saw you arrive from the villa. Shall we . . . ?' He turned towards the quay, where the *Conqueror* was moored. 'We're on a tight schedule.'

Jake looked back towards the slaves' enclosure. The young girl was being unchained and handed over to the man with the white beard in exchange for a number of gold coins.

'Unpleasant, I know,' said Charlie quietly, ushering

him forward, 'but these times are different. You'll need to get used to that. Besides' – he indicated the buyer – 'he looks kind. Her life might even take a turn for the better.'

Jake reluctantly tore his gaze away and followed Nathan back to the ship. Rose jumped down onto the pier when she saw them coming. 'Thank God you're safe!' she said, kissing them in the continental way with a peck on either cheek. Mr Drake, on Charlie's shoulder, edged away distastefully. 'So where's old misery?' she asked, looking expectantly around for Jupitus.

'Mr Cole is at the villa,' Nathan muttered through gritted teeth, 'mining every last drop of sympathy from his dreadful state.'

'And what exactly is his dreadful state?' Rose asked nervously.

'You'll see when you get there. I'm afraid he has selected you to look after him while the three of us continue on to Vulcano.'

Jake felt an immediate thrill at the notion of *the three of us*: whatever the mission was going to be, he was now part of it. 'So what happened to the *Hippocampus*?' he asked.

Charlie briefly recounted the terrible events of

the storm and how they were nearly drowned. When he had finished, Rose shook her head and took a deep breath. 'Dear me, did no one check the storm records?'

Nathan couldn't resist smirking. 'Good question.'

Charlie was, as always, diplomatic. 'Mr Cole, I gather, was rather preoccupied before he left, so the oversight was understandable.'

'I love it!' Rose trilled. '*Not* that you had such a terrible time,' she added quickly, 'but that the infallible Jupitus Cole actually messed up.'

'Anyway,' Charlie continued, 'it took three days and *all* my ingenuity to fix the Meslith machine, which is why you didn't hear from us for so long. And, most amazing of all, the *Hippocampus* will sail again.'

Nathan pointed along the docks towards a warehouse. 'They're rebuilding her down there as we speak. That's your other job, Miss Djones: to keep an eye on progress. They should be finished by the end of the week.'

'It sounds like I'm on holiday,' Rose announced happily. 'So where is this famous villa?'

'Follow that path all the way to the top . . .' Nathan pointed to a flight of steps. 'It's the double

151

doors surrounded by bougainvillea. And good luck.'
He turned to Jake. 'So, you ready to set sail again?'

'Absolutely!' Jake found himself replying with a
salute, much to Charlie's consternation.

'Please don't encourage him,' he said, casting his
bag onto the deck of the *Conqueror*. 'He already
thinks he's God.'

Before the agents went their separate ways, Rose
produced the hoisting device that Dr Chatterju had
given her – the belt with the lion-shaped buckle –
and handed it to Nathan.

'My invention!' he exclaimed when he realized
what it was. 'Chatterju is a genius!' he added,
immediately substituting it for his current belt and
attaching his scabbard.

The three young agents all said their goodbyes to
Rose, boarded the *Conqueror*, and cast off. Nathan
confidently weaved his way through to open water.
As Charlie unfurled the new map of the Tyrrhenian
Sea, Jake watched his aunt head up the steps until
she had disappeared from sight.

Rose followed the path all the way up, along narrow,
sun-baked passageways that cut between the jigsaw
of houses, until the air freshened and the bustle of

the town was left behind. From within the houses she could now hear the sounds of lunch being prepared.

'Ah, the bougainvillea.' She smiled as a shock of flaming pink came into view. The flowers tumbled around an old doorway. Rose turned the bronze handle, opened the door (it was ancient, even for AD 27, and creaked tantalizingly) and went inside. She sighed with delight as she found herself in the spacious, untamed gardens of a handsome villa. On all sides, a series of crumbling terraces, each lined with pots of sweet-smelling flowers, teetered down the side of the hill. The sound of trickling water came from a number of little fountains and ponds. There was also the most spectacular view of the harbour, the bay beyond and the perfect blue sea.

Rose looked around for any sign of life. 'Jupitus? Are you there?' she asked quietly, more to herself than anyone else. Then she spied a figure seated in the shade of a loggia. As she approached, she saw that the person's right leg was entirely encased in plaster and rested on a stool. The remaining flesh on show was a ghostly shade of alabaster – unmistakably belonging to Jupitus Cole. Assuming that he was fast asleep, Rose approached on tiptoe.

'I can hear you, Rosalind,' Jupitus murmured, without turning his head. 'A herd of bison galumphing towards me couldn't be less subtle.'

Momentarily Rose bristled with anger, but when she realized what a sorry state he was in, she softened. 'You'll have to be nice to me,' she said with a twinkle in her eye, 'otherwise I won't make you lunch.'

He shrugged without removing his gaze from the ocean. 'Already had lunch.'

'Well, you'll have to be nice to me anyway,' she replied in a firmer, steadier tone.

Now he did look up at her, with eyes that were proud and sad at the same time, and with the tiniest glimmer of a smile. 'It suits you, your hair like that, Rosalind,' he said quietly. 'Quite romantic.'

And he turned his gaze back to the sea.

9 THE SHADOW'S HAND

'So, AD 27 – how much do you know about it?' Charlie asked.

Jake shrugged. 'Well, the usual amount, I suppose . . .'

'I see – basically not a lot?'

They were standing at the prow in the shadow of the sail. Nathan was still at the helm, his head tilted towards the sun and a makeshift collar of shiny metal around his neck to maximize his tan.

'How much do you know about ancient Rome in general?' Charlie continued.

'I know about Julius Caesar,' Jake began excitedly. 'He was murdered.'

'Yes, in the Theatre of Pompey, by his fellow senators – though that was over seventy years ago now. Do you know *why* he was murdered?'

Jake replied with a gesture somewhere between a nod and a shake. He quite liked it when Charlie acted like an eccentric schoolteacher, but was also a little scared.

'Because he wanted to rule Rome all by himself. In short, he wanted to be *king*,' Charlie explained.

'I see,' Jake murmured wisely.

'But Rome hated the idea of a king, a single ruler. For hundreds of years it had been what they called a *republic*, with a new government elected every year. So they killed Julius Caesar.' Charlie demonstrated with a little mime of being stabbed a number of times. It was disconcerting enough for Mr Drake to go flying off in a huff and resettle on the yardarm. 'The trouble was, Julius Caesar had convinced so many people that a king – or rather an *emperor*, as they called it – would be good idea that it was too late to go back to the old ways. Anyway, to cut a long story short, there were seventeen years of exceedingly bloody civil war, some very gory decapitations and so on and so forth – until eventually Caesar's son, Augustus, became the first true emperor of Rome.'

'Quite a man, Augustus,' Nathan chipped in as he rearranged his sun reflector.

'Very accomplished indeed,' Charlie concurred. 'He expanded the Roman Empire dramatically, to Egypt and North Africa and east to Macedonia, connecting it all with hundreds of roads, as well as completely rebuilding Rome itself, transforming it – in his own words – *from a city of bricks to a city of marble.*'

'So is he still the emperor?' Jake asked.

'Died thirteen years ago,' Charlie replied. 'His stepson, Tiberius, is now in charge.'

'Bit of a tricky one, Tiberius,' Nathan put in.

'Nathan's right. He was once a good general, but he never really wanted the job of emperor, which explains why he now lives as a recluse on the island of Capri, governing at a remove through his right-hand man Lucius Sejanus, another gruff army type.'

'At a remove?' queried Jake.

'By post,' Charlie clarified. 'He rules the entire Roman Empire by letter.'

'But make no mistake' – Nathan left the helm and approached the others, holding out his arms dramatically and speaking in his most theatrical tones – 'Rome is in its heyday, rich beyond belief, huge armies everywhere; the greatest, most powerful civilization the world has ever known.'

157

'I'm sorry . . .' Charlie shook his head. 'I can't take you seriously in that ridiculous collar.'

'What?' Nathan shrugged. 'You'd prefer an untanned neck? Like some barbarian? Romans are very judgemental, very body conscious. You get things even slightly wrong and you're a laughing stock. Besides, I have standards, Charlie Chieverley.' He stuck out his chin and retreated back to the helm.

'You? A laughing stock?' Charlie shook his head at Jake. 'Surely not possible?'

Jake smiled to himself: he'd missed the friendly banter between the two of them. As he stared out to sea, he found himself standing straighter, his shoulders back, proud to be on a mission with his friends again. Then his mind turned to their assignment: to find Topaz St Honoré. Out of the blue she had sent that Meslith to Point Zero with her time and place coordinates – the island of Vulcano in May, AD 27 – along with the coded phrase: *Follow the shadow's hand.*

Topaz had haunted Jake's thoughts every day since she disappeared into the foaming waters of the North Sea. Her image sometimes appeared to him smiling or laughing – like on the day they first met in London, or at the village dance by the Rhine in

Germany. At other times she lurked in shadows, lost, full of sadness, a prisoner of her own dreadful history. Although she had been brought up – since the age of five – by Nathan's family on the Mont St Michel, she was actually related by blood to one of the History Keepers' greatest enemies, the diabolical Zeldt family. Daughter of Agata, she was also the niece of Xander, the prince who had plotted in vain to destroy the Renaissance.

By early afternoon an island had come into view ahead. 'That'll be it,' Charlie commented. 'Vulcano, the most southern of the Aeolian Islands.' He raised his telescope to examine it, then passed it over. Jake surveyed Vulcano with keen interest: it was maybe eight miles across, with sheer cliffs, and so thickly wooded it appeared like a giant emerald rising up out of the sea.

'Quite an odd destination – it's barely populated, with just one little port,' Charlie said, pointing towards a cluster of houses at the base of a steep slope, 'servicing various mining outfits. Even the volcano is dormant. Of course, like everywhere in the Roman world, there are all sorts of local stories: some say the island is the chimney from Vulcan's workshop, others that it's the entrance to the underworld.'

At the word 'underworld', Jake noticed Nathan giving Charlie a nervous glance.

As the *Conqueror* glided into the bay, Jake noticed a smell – a pungent, sour stench – which grew stronger as they approached. He looked round at Nathan, whose face was screwed up with distaste.

'Dear me, Charlie,' the American drawled. 'Have you been at the lentils again? I thought we discussed that.'

'It's sulphur, you idiot,' Charlie retorted. 'It's obviously one of the minerals they excavate here. Look . . .' He pointed to crates full of yellowish stone. 'Along with charcoal by the look of it,' he added with a nod towards a mound of black rocks.

The sulphur was a little too much for Nathan, who took out a silk handkerchief and held it to his nose.

As they docked at the makeshift wooden quay, various sullen-looking locals, their faces dirty from the mines, watched them through narrow, suspicious eyes.

'Friendly looking bunch,' Nathan commented under his breath.

Charlie, who was never one to take hostility personally, disembarked and cheerily approached a particularly grim-faced group; they looked like they might tear him in two and eat him for tea, but he simply bade them good morning, showed them his map and questioned them at length – needless to say, he was the only one of the agents who could speak and understand Latin with real fluency. The miners replied with a lot of grunting and ominous shaking of heads. Once he had found out what he wanted to know, Charlie returned to the others.

'Right, I think I have deciphered everything. Apparently Topaz's coordinates refer to a small temple, an hour's walk up the mountain. It's been deserted for decades, but was originally dedicated to Proserpina, the Roman goddess of the underworld.' Once again Nathan shot Charlie that look of trepidation. 'Sometimes known as the "Queen of Shades", which is very interesting, given Topaz's message: *Follow the shadow's hands.* According to the legend,' Charlie explained, 'Proserpina was abducted by Pluto against her will, and her good-ness turned to evil, causing her mother, Ceres, to heap all sorts of revenge on mankind.'

'Yes, fascinating,' Nathan interrupted impatiently.

161

'Why were they all shaking their heads?'

'Oh, just some silly local story about the temple being haunted by the ghosts of her victims.'

'No!' Nathan suddenly exclaimed in a high-pitched voice that took Jake by surprise. 'Absolutely not! You know full well that I don't do ghosts in *any* form.' He shivered with horror. 'You two go alone. I'll wait here and keep my eye on the ship. Besides, the whole business is suspect – why would Topaz lead us to some derelict temple in the middle of nowhere? It makes no sense.'

'Which is precisely why we need to investigate,' insisted Charlie, fastening his cape. '*All* of us! Non-negotiable.'

A short while later, having left Mr Drake happily eating his lunch, Charlie led the way up the steep path towards the old temple. Jake noticed that Nathan was looking nervously from side to side. It was cool in the forest, out of the sun, and a scent of pine filled their nostrils. It was quiet apart from the occasional caw of a bird, but sometimes a twig would snap and Nathan would stop dead, staring into the dark canopy of trees, certain that some phantom was about to strike.

'If it was a ghost,' Charlie pointed out, pulling him on, 'you probably wouldn't hear it coming.'

'Thanks,' Nathan snorted. 'You really know how to put a man at his ease.'

Finally they emerged from under the trees and rounded a rocky peak. Gradually the terrain flattened out. It was an even more unsettling place than the forest. An otherworldly stillness hung in the air; the soil was black and dry, and giant boulders of pumice lay strewn about amongst gnarled, dead trees. Nathan became even more jittery, and when the temple finally loomed up ahead – two crumbling, lopsided columns framing a dark opening – the blood drained from his face entirely.

'This has got to be some kind of mistake . . .' He shook his head. 'Why don't we check Topaz's coordinates again?'

Charlie ignored him and headed for the doorway. A flight of cracked stone steps descended into darkness.

Nathan kept his distance. 'Well, what can you see?' he asked nervously.

'*Ssh*,' Charlie ordered. 'I can hear something . . .' He listened intently. 'Something . . . or *someone*.'

'Who?' Nathan gulped. 'What can you hear?'

Charlie continued in a low whisper, 'Lost souls . . . I can hear them calling. They're saying . . .'

'What are they saying?'

'A man approaches who poses danger to all; a man of strong physique, of limitless vanity.'

Nathan screwed up his face, listening for the voices, but heard nothing but the wind swirling out of the dark opening.

'A man who thinks that ultramarine makes his eyes really pop. Bring us the head of Nathan Wylder—'

'Shut up, Charlie, just shut up! That's an order. We all have our little foibles. You don't like goat's cheese or unpunctuality, so please respect my one tiny little phobia.'

'Look, why don't we all go in together?' Jake suggested, trying to suppress a smile. 'I'll take your arm if you like.' If he was honest, Jake was frightened too – the whistling of that wind did sound ghostly – but he felt that they would get on quicker if he appeared as unbothered as Charlie. Under any other circumstance Nathan would never have accepted Jake's offer, but now he took his hand and squeezed it tight.

Charlie grabbed a fire torch from his holdall, lit it and set off.

'I'll take that, thank you very much.' Nathan swiped the light and followed closely behind, with Jake at his side.

Grit crunched underfoot as they went down the steps. The air became colder as they proceeded further into the mountainside, and the faint breeze continued to whistle eerily. Finally they found themselves in a chamber and looked around. It was not a sight to put Nathan at his ease. Even Charlie found his heart beating fast.

It was unexpectedly large – like a crypt under a big church – paved with great slabs of ancient black stone, with a ceiling that disappeared into the gloom above. At the far end, dominating the space and ominously watching any intruder, was a great statue on a pedestal.

'Our friend Proserpina, I take it,' Charlie said, adjusting his spectacles.

She was much larger than life size – a scowling warrior goddess, seated, but with clawed hands out-stretched as if she were about to tear her enemies apart.

Nathan was standing like a statue himself, clutching Jake's hand in a painful grip. Jake loosened his fingers a little before examining the rest of the room: set in recesses in the walls stood four much smaller statues, looking frail compared to the menacing goddess. Two lamps hung, unlit, from the ceiling, but otherwise the chamber was bare. There was a scurrying sound, and it was Jake's turn to freeze as a rat darted along the wall.

'I hate those creatures,' he muttered under his breath as he joined Charlie in front of the statue.

'This must be an antechamber,' Charlie said, watching the rat disappear through a hole in the corner. '*Follow the shadow's hands . . .*' he mused, peering at the goddess. 'Here – give me a leg up.'

Jake obliged, cupping his palms together and helping Charlie up onto the pedestal so that he was on a level with the statue's eyes. Carefully he examined Proserpina's fearsome hands to see if there was any movement in them. 'The hands must be the key – to let us in somewhere.'

Nathan tentatively advanced towards one of the smaller statues. He held up the torch and examined it in detail, his face wrinkling in disgust. Finely carved from stone, it looked like an emaciated corpse in a ghostly gown, with its head hanging down at an angle and stone worms crawling out of its eye sockets. As he looked closer, the head suddenly shot up and glared back at him. Nathan screamed, the torch went flying, and the whole room was plunged in darkness.

'Hell's bells! Nathan, what are you doing?' Charlie's voice shouted out.

'It moved! The statue moved – it looked right at me!' Nathan cried.

Jake had heard the torch drop and felt along the floor until he found it. He produced his flint lighter (ever since Nathan had given it to him on that dark night in sixteenth-century Venice he had never been without it) and re-lit it.

Nathan was cowering on the floor. 'You see?' he said, pointing at the statue. 'It was looking down before.'

As much as Charlie wanted to scoff at Nathan's silliness, he had to agree. 'Unbelievably, you're right . . .' He looked around at the other effigies. 'A moment ago all four of them were looking down; now only that one is.' As they turned to look, there was a grinding of stone and this last figure also lifted its grisly head.

'That's it, we're leaving,' said Nathan emphatically. 'There must be another way in to wherever we're going.'

'Just calm down!' Charlie told him. 'They're obviously *intended* to scare people and stop them coming down here. That's why it's said to be haunted.' To demonstrate his lack of concern, he went over and tapped one on its bony thigh. 'You see, just stone. Far more importantly, we need to find out how we get beyond this chamber – so please, could everyone put their heads together and work out what is meant by *follow the shadow's hand*.'

At this moment a long-lost memory surfaced in Jake's mind: one evening, when there was a power cut in his house (his dad, in a doomed attempt to create a built-in wardrobe in the hall, had accidentally drilled into the main fuse box), they had lit candles in the kitchen and Jake and his brother had made shadow puppets on the wall.

He looked over to the statue of Proserpina with her hands outstretched, and then at the two bronze lamps hanging from the ceiling. He went over to one of these and raised the torch as if to light it. To everyone's surprise, it ignited immediately. He went over and lit the other; this also lit up with a satisfying *whoomph*. Intrigued and perplexed, Charlie and Nathan stood watching as Jake went behind the statue and examined the back wall. 'There,' he said. '*The shadow's hand.*'

Nathan picked himself up, and he and Charlie went to look. They were astonished: the light from the lamps cast two sets of overlapping shadows, creating the image of a single large hand, its fore-finger pointing at one brick in particular – one out of thousands that made up the back wall.

It seemed obvious now. Jake put his finger to the brick – it was spongy to the touch – and pressed hard. A moment later there was a deep rasping sound, and the entire middle section of wall rose up, gradually revealing a secret space beyond.

'He'll be putting us out of a job soon,' said Charlie, giving Jake a clap on the back. Nathan was so impressed that for a moment he forgot all about his fear of ghosts.

Jake led the way in as Charlie wedged a stone in the opening so they wouldn't be trapped inside. All three squinted into the gloom. It was roughly the width of a London Underground tunnel, and criss-crossed by a network of gossamer cobwebs. At the far end, standing in an indistinct pool of light, they saw a hunched figure.

'That's either another statue . . . or someone standing very still,' Charlie whispered.

'So kind of you to put me out of my misery,' Nathan replied drily.

'Come on – let's go,' said Jake, forging on. He felt he was tantalizingly close to Topaz and there was not a moment to lose.

'Stop!' Charlie suddenly shouted and pulled him back. 'Look!' He pointed to a shape protruding from the wall: a stone carving of a dog's head with its mouth wide open for the kill.

'There's another one there,' said Jake, making out an identical form on the opposite wall. 'And there!' He nodded at a third one jutting down from the ceiling.

Charlie understood immediately. 'Of course – Cerberus, the three-headed dog who guards the entrance to the underworld. And like the real thing, I have a feeling that this one is not exactly amiable. Look in its mouth there.'

Jake and Nathan peered up into the inky black cavity between the jaws of the dog on the left-hand wall, and could just make out, in the place of its tongue, the faint glint of an arrowhead.

Charlie removed his cape, bundled it up and carefully pitched it forward to a point directly between the three heads. There was a collective *twang* and a sudden rush of air. Three glints of light converged, and the balled-up cloak dropped to the ground – with three arrows sticking out of it. Charlie picked it up, removed the darts, tossed them to one side and shook it out: it had several holes in it now. 'What do you reckon, Nathan? Fashionably distressed?'

Nathan rolled his eyes. 'I hate that look. I have not an iota of respect for it. I mean, honestly – randomly torn material? Where's the craftsmanship?'

Once again Jake was forging on, his eyes fixed on the stooped, still figure at the end of the tunnel. He stopped just short of it. Charlie's first guess was right: it was indeed a statue, but carved from wood, not stone. It reminded Jake of some ancient relic you might find in a cathedral – an old man with a haggard face just visible under his hood and cloak and a wizened hand reaching out, palm up. It stood – like a mast – in the centre of a small wooden boat, set across a channel that disappeared, at either end, into the mountain. In the shadows underneath lay pools of water.

'That will be Charon then,' said Charlie, increasingly impressed by the set-up. 'The ferryman to the underworld. Our hosts, whoever they may be, are certainly doing things thoroughly – although the River Styx has seen better days,' he added with a nod towards the damp channel. 'That's perfect . . .' He had spotted something else. 'There's a slot in the palm of his hand. You know how the legend goes, of course?' he said, turning to Jake. 'You have to pay the ferryman to take you across the Styx; otherwise you must wander in limbo for eternity.'

'Limbo for eternity . . .' mused Nathan. 'Sounds a bit like that trip you once forced me to go on – the cuckoo clocks of Switzerland.' Charlie ignored him, produced a single golden coin from his pocket and inserted it into the slot. 'Wait!' Nathan shouted. 'Discussion first, please.'

'Oops.' Charlie shrugged as he opened his fingers and let go. The three of them heard the coin roll down inside the arm and land with a clink.

Nothing happened for a moment; then, gradually, they became aware of a distant rumble of water. It reverberated from deep within the mountain, quickly getting closer and louder. Finally it started to flow along the channel – just a trickle at first, then a stream, and soon a foaming torrent. Charon's boat straightened and rose up from the bottom of the channel.

'Quickly – all aboard!' Charlie cried, jumping in. Jake followed excitedly, holding onto the rigid ferryman.

Nathan stood his ground, shaking his head. 'It seems to have slipped your minds that I'm in charge here and we haven't discussed this yet – who knows where that river might lead?' But it was pointless putting up a fight – their course was inevitable. 'Totally unprofessional . . .' he grunted, running after them and leaping aboard as the boat took off down the tunnel.

The three of them yelled, half with fear and half with delight, as it careered this way and that, plunging down through the mountain, under the unflinching eye of the wooden ferryman. At one point the tunnel levelled out and they slowed, almost coming to a halt; then it fell away again, and they went plummeting down.

They held onto Charon, mouths open in a nonstop howl as they tore along the final stretch before emerging into the light, at which point they slowed down and stopped. They stepped off and climbed a small flight of steps to see where they were.

They had found themselves in paradise.

10 THE HYDRA GUARD

The sun cast a golden light over a steep, verdant valley that led to a cliff high above the sea. In the middle stood a group of fine-looking buildings, all connected by magnificent gardens filled with brightly coloured flowers, lawns, terraces, colonnaded walkways and fountains. Occupying the prime position, looking out over the sparkling ocean, was a striking villa of white marble, surrounded by tall palm trees.

The whole place swarmed with activity. A small army of youngsters – tanned, healthy-looking and as fit as Olympians – were training in different areas of the camp. In a circular sandpit, two young men were engaged in a swordfight. Even from a distance, Jake could see that this was no casual sparring contest: they looked and sounded as if they were

174

fighting to the death. In other areas, youths practised boxing, archery and Roman martial arts. Those who weren't training sat on benches, watching attentively as they awaited their turn.

Further groups of attendants, workmen and gardeners – all wearing identical brown livery – busied themselves around the estate.

Jake, Nathan and Charlie, who had retreated into the shade between a cluster of trees and a small outbuilding, surveyed all this in silence. In vain, Jake had scanned the girls to see if Topaz was amongst them.

'A holiday camp?' Nathan drawled sarcastically as the vanquished gladiator was dragged limp and bloody from the sandpit.

'Nathan – look,' said Charlie, pointing to a towering structure – a giant domed cage, constructed from an intricate lattice of stone joists. Inside, several huge, vicious-looking birds glided around or sat on high perches. The dome itself was topped by a fearsome statue of a giant bird of prey, wings outstretched for flight. 'Vultures,' he said. 'Or, if I'm not mistaken, a particular type of vulture. Interbred with *Polemaetus bellicosus*, the martial eagle – one of the deadliest birds of prey on the planet – to make them extra bloodthirsty. Nathan and I have heard about these before, haven't we?'

'We certainly have.' Nathan scowled at the vast aviary. 'They're Agata Zeldt's pet of choice. The commander was right: this must be her hideaway.'

Once again, at the sound of Agata's name – *the most evil woman in history* – Jake felt his stomach flip over. She was the sister of Xander Zeldt, the dark prince from whom he had narrowly escaped in Germany. She was also Topaz's mother – although Topaz had disowned her entirely.

The Zeldt dynasty was the oldest enemy of the History Keepers. The mere mention of their name could terrify even the bravest agents. In the beginning, Rasmus Zeldt had been a friend and contemporary of Sejanus Poppoloe, the founder of the secret service; but he had descended into madness, disavowed the organization and pronounced himself king – not just of the world, but of time itself.

Many generations had come and gone before the monstrous King Sigvard had then appeared and declared war on all history, vowing to ruin the world and steep it in evil. He had taken a grand tour of the greatest atrocities of the past, from the Spanish

Inquisition to the witch hunts of Salem, learning his craft, before starting his own campaign of horror – attempting to destroy the past, to pick away at it and make the world unravel into a savage, ungodly place.

When he'd died unexpectedly on a campaign in ancient Mesopotamia, his children, Xander and Agata (Alric, his second son, had been missing for decades), had carried on his work with even greater zeal. For a whole generation, the History Keepers had fought them tirelessly, thwarting plot after plot. Three years ago, around the time that Jake's brother Philip had gone missing, they had disappeared from the scene; but recently Xander had resurfaced with a nightmarish scheme to destroy the Renaissance. He'd been vanquished and left, horribly burned, on his warship, the *Lindwurm*.

But now it seemed that his sister Agata might be up to no good.

'So, do we think that's her personal residence?' Nathan pointed to the white villa.

'That's where Topaz must be,' said Jake, scrutinizing its colonnades. 'What do we do next?'

'Men approaching, twelve o'clock.' Charlie nodded towards two attendants hurrying up the steps in their direction.

They quickly retreated to the other side of the outbuilding. Looking through a window, they realized that it was a laundry – there were vats of washing, as well as sheets and clothes hung up to dry. The two slaves went in, took some tunics from a pile – brown ones like their own – and left.

'Thinking what I'm thinking?' Nathan asked, leaping up onto the window ledge. He double-checked that the room was empty, reached in, grabbed three more uniforms and jumped back down. 'Look,' he said, showing them the stitching on the front of each. 'In case we needed more proof – *A* for Agata.' The letter was inscribed over the symbol of a swooping vulture, talons extended.

The three of them swiftly removed their own light tunics and slipped on the brown uniforms.

'The slave look isn't my bag at all,' Nathan complained, adjusting the cheap material to conceal his scabbard. 'Charlie Chieverley, what on earth have you got on?' he exclaimed. 'I do believe you have surpassed yourself.'

He was referring to the underwear that Charlie was trying but failing to keep hidden as he dressed – half-pantaloons embroidered with Roman figures.

'They're educational!' Charlie reddened as he yanked the new tunic down. 'They're my favourite characters from the ancient world: Aristotle, Archimedes, Cicero – to name but a few.'

He had only just sorted himself out when a stout man with a pockmarked face came round the building towards them, shouting something in Latin. At first Jake's heart stopped, thinking they had been rumbled, but it became clear that the man's annoyance was work-related: he wore the same brown tunic as the others, but seemed to be in charge. Charlie bowed and replied politely. Finally, the tirade over, the man strode off down the steps towards another unfortunate group of slaves.

'We have to take those baskets down to the laboratory immediately,' Charlie translated, once the man was out of earshot; he pointed to a stack of wicker baskets loaded with chunks of rock – the same pungent-smelling sulphur they had seen in the harbour. 'And he also let slip that the *magistra* – that's Agata Zeldt, I presume – is not presently in residence. That may be good or bad news. Quickly, we'd better move those rocks; we don't want to attract attention.'

They set to immediately, grabbing two baskets

179

apiece. As Jake lifted his, the cloying stench caught in the back of his throat, making him gag.

'Which do you think is the laboratory?' Nathan asked, trying not to breathe as he scanned the various buildings.

'There.' Jake nodded towards a low octagonal building, to which two workers were carrying similar loads.

They headed down the path towards it, passing close to the aviary. It was feeding time, and a man was shovelling great chunks of raw meat into a shoot that dropped down into the cage. The birds, which were almost as big as humans, flew down in a frenzy, cawing and scrapping as they tore off ribbons of flesh with their razor-sharp beaks.

'So what's the deal with sulphur?' Nathan asked. 'Any ideas, Charlie?'

Charlie shrugged. 'It could be used to make hundreds of things – medicines, pesticides, paper, vulcanizing rubber, sulphuric acid . . .'

Presently a gang of young warriors, pumped up after a bloody bout, came swaggering along the path towards them. They reminded Jake of a gang of hot-headed bullies at his school, only these were tough, muscular fighting machines. Close up, Jake could see their uniform more clearly: each wore a pale-grey moulded leather breastplate, with feathers sprouting from the shoulders. More feathers decorated the backs of their thick gladiator's boots. To complete the bird-of-prey theme, two of the guards were wearing glinting bronze masks with slit-like eyeholes and an armoured nose, hooked like a vulture's; the others were carrying theirs.

The three young agents kept their heads down as they passed by, but Jake noticed that one of the guards – he had a chiselled face and a dimple in his chin – was watching them through narrowed eyes.

As they carried on down the series of steps and paths towards the hexagonal building, Jake, heart thumping, continued to scan all the female faces in the hope of glimpsing Topaz; but she was nowhere to be seen.

They went in and found themselves in a large room. It was dim and cool – and empty. The air was thick with the most dreadful odour – not just the sulphur, but something even more acrid. There were several work benches covered in gleaming bronze instruments, scales and measuring cups as well as jars of specimens, liquids and powders.

'I assume the revolting whiff comes from those

dreadful things over there,' said Nathan, pointing to an array of curious plants along one wall. Each bore a huge flower shaped like a colourless, giant tongue protruding from deep indigo petals.

'*Amorphophallus titanium.*' Charlie nodded in agreement. 'Corpse flowers, as they are charmingly known. As well as smelling like putrefying flesh, they actually contain a stomach that can eat a small rodent. More and more, I'm endeared to our hostess.'

A man appeared through another door; he headed for a work bench and started pounding something with a pestle and mortar. He was tall and thin, with an angular face and a long plaited beard. Barely glancing at the boys, he indicated that they should deposit their baskets in the corner. They set them carefully down next to a stack of crates filled with crumbling pieces of rock. Jake caught sight of some unusual glass containers, hexagonal in shape – like the building – and filled to the brim with a blackish powder.

However, the bearded man now dismissed them with a brusque clap of his hands and they were forced to turn round and leave the building. On the other side of a stone courtyard was the main villa. A group of uniformed slaves were filing in through a side door.

'That's where we're heading next,' said Nathan. 'The key is to look like we know what we're doing.' With that, he took a deep breath and set off across the courtyard, the others following close behind. They checked that no one was watching and slipped through the side door into a dark passageway that ran the length of the house. At the other end, the slaves were just turning the corner, their feet softly echoing on the stone floor, and were soon out of sight.

The boys passed a doorway that led to a central atrium and peered in. It was as wide, high and bright as the service areas were cramped and dark, with a grand staircase and floors paved in white marble.

Nathan signalled for them to continue along the passage. 'This way for the private suites, I would say,' he whispered, and they headed up the staircase. As they did so, they failed to notice two heavy-set figures watching from the end of the corridor.

Coming to a door, Nathan signalled for silence and carefully unsheathed his sword. He opened it and peered inside, then motioned for the others to follow.

They found themselves in a lady's dressing room. Jake wondered if he might finally set eyes on Topaz, until Charlie announced, 'Agata's quarters – look.' He pointed to a dressing table, its base resembling another monstrous bird of prey. The bird motif was everywhere: on the handle of a vanity mirror, in a ceiling fresco, pictured on the lids of coloured glass jars of perfumes and make-up.

A short passageway led to the bedroom. Again Nathan, weapon at the ready, gingerly advanced and, finding it empty, signalled for Jake and Charlie to follow.

The room was dominated by a throne-like bed illuminated by rays of late-afternoon sun streaming through two huge windows – glassless frames with a single horizontal bar – that looked out across the ocean. The room was empty, but there were signs of recent occupancy: the bed had been stripped, but the bedclothes still lay in a heap on the floor; a chest had been emptied and its drawers left open.

Nathan clicked his fingers at Jake. 'Stand over there – make sure no one's coming,' he ordered. Jake went over to the main door. It was slightly ajar and he had a view of the landing and the top of the staircase.

Meanwhile Nathan headed over to the window and looked down at the vertiginous drop. 'Ouch,' he whistled. 'Quite a plummet.'

Charlie examined some large scrolls that had been unrolled on a desk and held down with weights. On top was an ancient map of Europe, Asia and Africa; the continents were oddly shaped but distinguishable. A great swathe, from the Atlantic, across the Mediterranean and North Africa, and all the way to the Persian Gulf, was coloured red.

'The extent of the Roman Empire?' Nathan asked.

'In theory,' sighed Charlie. 'Though our friend Agata seems to be staking a claim.' He referred to her symbol of a vulture emblazoned with an A that was printed on every country pictured.

From where Jake was standing, he could see only a mass of red spread across the page. As he craned his head round to get a better view, he noticed something lying on the floor – a single sheet of parchment that had got caught under his foot. He picked it up and examined it. It looked like the title page of a manuscript: there was a single heading, scrawled in ink – *Counters* – and below this, a motif of seven golden eggs. Jake wondered if it was important.

'Guys,' he whispered over to the others, 'what do you think about this?' There was no reply. 'Guys . . . ?' he called again.

Neither Nathan nor Charlie was listening. They had seen something shocking.

'Is that who I think it is?' Nathan asked. He was referring to a painting set into an alcove: it depicted a young man – arrogant, haughty, with a mane of perfectly straight blond hair.

'The Leopard!' Charlie gasped in astonishment.

11 Exit Paradise

Jake's breath stopped at the sound of the name. *The Leopard* – the vile, silky-voiced spy who had intercepted them at the Stockholm opera house; the man whose accomplice Jake had woefully mistaken for Philip; the enemy agent who had made off with their entire consignment of atomium.

From the doorway, Jake turned round to look at it. Even from the other end of the room, the sneer was unmistakable.

'No, that really is too much,' Nathan declared as he set eyes on a companion portrait in an adjacent alcove. 'Why is Topaz next to that idiot?'

At the sound of her name, Jake abandoned his post, unaware of the two shadows moving up the stairs towards the landing, and was drawn irresistibly to the second picture. It was unmistakably her – the sphinx-like face, the indigo eyes, the tumbling tresses of golden hair. He could see that it had been painted recently; she still had the desperate look of a trapped animal that he had seen on the *Lindwurm*. This was bad enough, but there was an even greater shock: the two subjects were unmistakably similar. The Leopard (or rather *Leopardo*, as his name was given below the portrait) had the same mouth, the same cheekbones, the same eyes as Topaz.

Jake found himself asking a question to which he didn't really want to know the answer: 'Are they related, do you think?'

Charlie looked round at Nathan. 'What do you think? Could she have a brother we didn't know about?'

Nathan said nothing – just stared grimly at the portraits, his jaw clenched.

The discovery had set Charlie's mind racing. 'I hate to be the one to suggest it, but do you think she told him something about the Isaksens? Obviously she wouldn't have known about the rendezvous in Sweden, but it's an odd coincidence: *she* disappears and suddenly *he's* in Sweden.'

'Charlie, you're not thinking straight,' Nathan

pointed out. 'The Zeldts already knew about the Isaksens – they've known about them for centuries. Besides,' he added, almost angrily, 'there are no circumstances under which Topaz would talk, not even under duress.'

'*Omittite arma!*' shouted a voice from the doorway.

All three turned to see two muscular guards – gladiators from the training camp, both armed with swords. In an instant, the History Keepers had drawn their own weapons, though Jake got his caught up in his tunic.

'*Omittite arma!*' the first guard repeated.

'You want us to drop our weapons?' Nathan drawled as the men advanced. 'You're going to have to ask more politely than that.'

Suddenly two doors concealed behind the portraits crashed open and six more soldiers swept in. Jake froze, not knowing which way to turn, his sword still tangled up. Charlie swung round, but was caught off guard and was disarmed immediately. Nathan put up a brave fight, parrying the swords of his attackers – but the numbers were against him and within seconds four blades had converged on his head simultaneously. They hovered, glinting, in front of his eyes.

189

'I suppose that's as polite as it's going to get.' He shrugged, still refusing to surrender his weapon. With a sharp rap to his knuckles, one of the guards smashed it out of his hand. Jake finally freed his own weapon and, though the battle was surely lost, pointed it defiantly at each soldier in turn, edging towards the door.

He stopped when his back came into contact with something sharp. He turned slowly to see a *ninth* soldier. Jake recognized him as the youth with the dimpled chin who had watched them so intently when they passed by earlier. On impulse he lunged, but the boy quickly caught Jake's hand in his own huge paw, eyeballing him with a strange intensity as he removed the weapon from his grasp.

The History Keepers were herded together and led out of the room, the new arrival guarding their rear. Jake was horrified at himself: once again he had let his friends down. If he had stayed guarding the entrance, they might have had time to escape.

As they crossed the landing and started down the stairs, the ninth soldier shouted out to his comrades. They turned round, clearly perplexed; then, out of the blue, the dimpled youth shunted Jake and the others out of the way, pulled back his fist and punched the first guard with full force on the jaw. The man's neck cracked; disbelief flashed in his eyes as he teetered and fell, toppling the entire platoon like a set of skittles. Like a giant snowball rolling out of control, they somersaulted down the steps in a confusion of flying limbs, ankles twisting, skulls cracking, flecks of blood spattering over the white marble.

'Topaz friends?' the mutineer asked in a thick accent as he picked up the weapons dropped by one of his comrades. The boys were struck dumb, but Charlie managed to hold up a shaking hand. 'Lucius Titus,' the youth announced, flashing his perfect white teeth and firmly shaking each of them by the hand. 'I have waiting for you.' He returned their swords to them. 'Follow me. We have little time.' And he was off down the passageway.

'Where is Topaz?' Jake called after him.

'Quickly!' the soldier hissed as he disappeared round a corner.

'Who did he say he was?' Nathan asked. 'He looks rather pleased with himself.'

Charlie shrugged. 'Lucius Titus?'

In the hall below, Jake saw one of the fallen guards lift his bleeding head, fumble for a whistle and blow hard into it. He needn't have bothered: the front door was already flying open and another group of soldiers marched in.

'We should probably follow the man,' Charlie decided, and they hurried off along the passageway.

Lucius was waiting for them. 'Quickly now!' he ordered, herding them through a door, slamming it behind them and bolting it top and bottom. They found themselves in another bedroom like Agata's, but smaller. Lucius opened a chest, produced two long lengths of rope and started tying the end of one to the iron bar across the window.

'Is Topaz here?' Jake asked.

Nathan added airily, 'We'd love to have a word with her.'

'Gone, with the magistra.'

'The magistra?' Nathan repeated. 'I take it he means the delightful Agata?' he enquired of Charlie. 'The Zeldts do love their vulgar titles.'

'Gone where?' Jake enquired, a slight desperation creeping into his voice.

Lucius tightened the knot, threw the rope out of the window and began fastening the end of the second.